"You, lady, are a blue blood."

Doyle could hardly reign in his temper any longer. "Maybe you don't think about the differences but they're there."

But Leigh wasn't listening to him. She was staring down at the ground, her booted foot poking at something half-buried in the muck. She bent to retrieve it.

"There are ways that I can make you listen, Leigh," Doyle said in a predatory tone, taking a step closer.

He knew she wouldn't dare meet his eyes. She was busy unfolding a muddy piece of paper that had been crumpled into a ball.

"What the hell is that?" Doyle asked. Then he noted the color, and his pulse roared to life.

Frantic eyes scanning its contents, Leigh said, "A threat."

ABOUT THE AUTHOR

Patricia Rosemoor has always loved horses. While she no longer rides regularly, she continues to follow the careers of the finest thoroughbreds in the racing industry. On her first visit to the Kentucky Bluegrass area, she was privileged to see the behind-the-scenes workings of several horse farms. On her second visit, she was caught up in the melee of the Kentucky Derby. The love and devotion of the people who work with these four-legged athletes inspired this story.

Books by Patricia Rosemoor

HARLEQUIN INTRIGUE

38—DOUBLE IMAGES
55—DANGEROUS ILLUSIONS
74—DEATH SPIRAL
81—CRIMSON HOLIDAY
95—AMBUSHED
113—DO UNTO OTHERS
161—PUSHED TO THE LIMIT*
163—SQUARING ACCOUNTS*
165—NO HOLDS BARRED*
199—THE KISS OF DEATH

*Quid Pro Quo trilogy

Dead Heat

Patricia Rosemoor

Harlequin Books

TORONTO • NEW YORK • LONDON
AMSTERDAM • PARIS • SYDNEY • HAMBURG
STOCKHOLM • ATHENS • TOKYO • MILAN
MADRID • WARSAW • BUDAPEST • AUCKLAND

To the winners and the contenders and all those
who dare to dream of being the best

Acknowledgments

I would like to thank the many organizations and their employees who contributed to my
knowledge of the Kentucky thoroughbred racing industry: Churchill Downs, the Kentucky
Derby Museum, the Keeneland library, TOBA (Thoroughbred Owners and Breeders
Association) and the farms—Spendthrift, Dixiana, Chesapeake and Gainesway.

Additional thanks to the Illinois organizations that got me started: Arlington International
Racecourse, Hill 'n Dale Farm and The Daily Racing Form.

Harlequin Intrigue edition published September 1993

ISBN 0-373-22243-2

DEAD HEAT

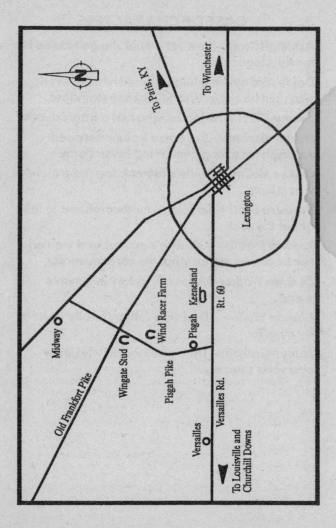

CAST OF CHARACTERS

Ashleigh Scott—How far would she go to keep her family's legacy?

Doyle McCoy—Ashleigh rubbed him the wrong way, but his gut instinct told him to stay close.

Jimmy Diaz—The jockey who met a tragic death.

Harley Barnett—This horse trainer despised Ashleigh for taking over Wind Racer Farm.

Oakes McCoy—Doyle's father knew more than he was telling.

Vanessa Scott—Ashleigh's mother refused to talk about the past.

Keith Wingate—Ashleigh's ex-husband wanted her back—no matter what the consequences.

Desiree Walker—A female jockey in a man's world.

Claude Walker—Desiree's father, fatally injured by a horse.

Lamar Graspin—The horse bookie who knew everyone's secrets.

Chapter One

Jimmy Diaz was spitting mad and ready to do battle. The old man could be a real pain in the butt at times— but *this!*

Jimmy would never have expected it of him.

He gave the note one last look-see and crushed it in his fist. Crumpling the damning paper felt good, but dropping it and grinding it under his heel into the muck where it belonged felt even better.

No way would he let this insult go!

Straightening to his full five feet four inches, Jimmy set off to meet the old bastard and give him what for.

WALKING ACROSS the Keeneland paddock area, Doyle McCoy spotted Lamar Graspin rushing from the backside where the horses were stabled, and he felt the wad of money burning a hole in his trouser pocket.

Doyle could hardly believe the old bookie still had the guts to work right out of the track whenever it suited him, usually at the biggest-stakes races like today's. The racing commission and the local police frowned on that sort of activity, but so far as Doyle knew, Lamar had never actually done time. He had dealt with the old bookie nearly twenty years before, when he'd been wet behind the ears and too young to be allowed to place a track bet.

Lamar disappeared into the grandstand area and Doyle turned his attention to the walking ring, where the horses in the next race were paraded around for the spectators' inspection. The jockeys in their colorful patterned silks were just getting a leg up onto their mounts' backs. Anticipation crackled through the warm mid-April air as the outrider led the parade of frisky fillies down the red-rubber-brick road, under the grandstand and out onto the track itself.

The wad in Doyle's pocket spoke to him louder. He was tempted to put a c-note on four to win. A long shot with—he checked the tote board—thirty-to-one odds. But something told him Lady Jane had it in her to go the distance, to fight it out with Dancing Dawn, his professional pick for this race.

As usual, he was tempted.

And, as usual, he left the money right where it was, a reminder of things gone wrong, nothing more. Proof that his interest could be engaged without him having to do anything about it. When a man grew up in Kentucky on the backside of a track, putting a few bucks on the ponies once in a while was only natural. Not that his ex-wife had seen it that way. Now she was gone and so were his kids. They'd found a replacement for him, a new home in Virginia and a new improved life.

Now Doyle's life *was* the track. Rather, lots of tracks. As a syndicated handicapper and racing columnist for the *Louisville Envoy* and a bunch of other papers, he got around, not only to Kentucky's finest—Keeneland and Churchill Downs—but, depending on the season, to Saratoga and Gulfstream and Santa Anita, as well. All the posh tracks for the rich and famous, and the blue bloods whose own lineage was as important to them as that of the thoroughbreds they raced.

Speaking of blue bloods...

He spotted Ashleigh Scott mincing her way across the paddock area in too-high yellow heels, the exact shade of her too-wide-brimmed yellow straw hat. A silk swath of purple flowers on a yellow background enveloped her soft curves and swirled around her long legs. She was surrounded by an entourage of two equally overdressed Southern belles and escorted by a gentleman in a dark suit and a white-on-white starched shirt.

Doyle couldn't help himself. He stepped directly in front of her and grinned, his gaze fastening on the small mole below the left corner of her mouth. "Why, Ash, darlin', don't you look pretty as a picture."

Her obliging smile was a mere shade away from feral. He knew she hated the nickname he'd given her as a kid—she preferred Ashleigh or Leigh, depending on which side of the racetrack was doing the calling. He also knew she'd prefer he drop off the face of the earth rather than call her anything at all.

"Why, Doyle McCoy, how *nice* to see you."

Nice indicating he belonged in the earth with the rest of the worms. Any Kentucky woman worth her salt could sound as though she was lavishing a man with compliments while grinding him under her dainty heel.

"Why don't y'all go on to the box without me," she told her friends.

They moved off, the pretty blonde staring at him over her shoulder. Doyle winked at her. The blonde giggled and hurried to keep up with her friends. And Doyle turned his attention back to Leigh. "I noticed Wind Racer has a couple of horses running today."

Wind Racer Farm being the Scott legacy, which, as an only child, Leigh would someday inherit from her mother, Vanessa.

"Yes, the Blue Grass Stakes is the highlight of the day, of course. But I do have a filly in this next race and I wouldn't think of missing Dancing Dawn win." She glanced toward the clubhouse, which her friends were just now entering. Her thick dark hair was pulled back from her fine features and gathered with a purple ribbon at the nape of her long, graceful neck—a neck that tempted a man's lips to assault of the very personal kind.

Not *his* lips, though.

When Doyle realized Leigh was staring at him openly, her thick-lashed eyes more brilliant than the Kentucky bluegrass and her guard relaxed for once, he couldn't stop himself from spoiling the moment. "Hmm, I thought Lady Jane looked pretty good myself."

Her jaw tightened but a smile remained attached to her lovely lips. "You always do make *interesting* choices when it comes to fillies."

"Part of my job."

But Doyle knew she meant the human kind of filly, like his high school sweetheart, who eloped with a traveling salesman two weeks before they were to graduate. Only thirteen at the time, Leigh had volunteered to be Betty's replacement. She hadn't taken kindly to his rebuff, no matter that he'd tried to let her down gently.

"Since you're so enamored of Lady Jane," Leigh was saying, "it's too bad you predicted in print Dancing Dawn would win, isn't it?"

With that shot, she strolled off, her shiny waterfall of dark hair undulating down her back like a horse's tail. Doyle stared after her. So she read his column, did she? He wondered if she would ever have admitted to doing so if she hadn't been trying to best him.

He and Ashleigh Scott had disrespected and disavowed each other for as long as Doyle could remember—starting sometime after he'd put an end to her romantic schoolgirl yearnings. The five-year gap in their ages had made any relationship other than friendship a no-no, of course. But they would have made an inappropriate match for other reasons, as well. She'd been too young to understand or accept the class/money structure that placed them in two different worlds.

At the time, his father had been working as a groom for her parents on Wind Racer Farm. Somehow, back then, the concept of inappropriateness had been lost on her.

But as they always did, things changed.

Leigh disappeared into the clubhouse, and Doyle's grin faded. He really had been fond of the kid who'd liked being called Ash all those years ago. It was a shame what she'd grown up to become—a real Bluegrass blue blood, nose just a tad too high in the air, sights set equally high no matter if the prize were a purse or a potential husband.

Yep, Doyle McCoy had no doubts that Ashleigh Scott considered herself too good for the likes of him or any man who grew up on the wrong side of the racetrack.

LEIGH FUMED AS SHE MADE her way to the Wind Racer box, where her friends would be waiting for her. She was angry because she couldn't instantly erase Doyle McCoy from her mind. Not that she was still taken in by his rugged good looks or rough-edged charm. She wasn't thirteen anymore, for heaven's sake.

The starting-gate bell shrilled, echoing through the clubhouse.

Leigh rushed by people turning from the betting windows. She cursed the fact that unlike any other major racetrack, Keeneland had no announcer calling the race.

Yells and screams of encouragement mixed with the thundering of hooves hitting dirt track. The crowd kept getting in her way, as if fate was determined to keep her from seeing this race on anything but an impersonal video monitor. A moment later, Leigh huffed into the box and picked up a pair of binoculars she'd left on her seat. The horses were already approaching the second turn.

"I didn't think you were going to make it," Jennifer said.

The blonde's voice held a teasing note that aggravated Leigh, who immediately looked through the binoculars. But instead of horses, she imagined she saw a thick crop of dark chestnut hair and hazel eyes that always seemed to mock her.

"Damn!" she muttered, trying to regain her composure and switch her attention away from the crass handicapper and back to where it belonged.

Why did Doyle McCoy always make her do a slow burn?

"What's wrong?" Nolan asked. "Isn't Dawn where she's supposed to be at this point in the race?"

"She's doing just fine." Leigh only prayed she wasn't fibbing. Dancing Dawn was smack-dab in the center of the pack as the fillies rounded the second turn and came down the stretch.

The audience rose *en masse* to watch the final seconds of the race as the jockeys made their moves for position and several of the mounts finally fired.

Leigh noted Lady Jane was leading by a head, and Angelbright was a close second. . . .

She watched closely as a chestnut filly whose jockey wore yellow-and-purple silks broke from the pack and began passing the other horses. Blood rushed straight to her head, making her dizzy with tension. Screams of excitement pierced the air around her, and Leigh wanted to scream, too. Miss Phipps, her old dancing-school teacher, would have had the vapors at such a tacky idea.

"Dancing Dawn is making her move!" Jennifer cried.

Leigh couldn't help it—she lost her composure. "C'mon, Dawn!" she shouted, praying for a victory and the purse the farm so very much needed.

She lowered the binoculars, her grip still tight as she watched Dancing Dawn pull ahead of Angelbright, then surge past Lady Jane to the finish line, leading by a mere neck.

"It's Dancing Dawn!" Nolan cried. "She did it!"

Leigh screamed and jumped up and down, so out of control that she almost let the binoculars fly. As she celebrated, she realized another of her companions— also a dancing-school graduate of Miss Phipps's—was arching a brow at the display. Leigh forced herself to settle down and gave Harmony an embarrassed grin.

The redhead smiled broadly and gave her a big hug and a pat on the back. "Oh, Ashleigh, what a precious filly!"

Giddy with happiness, Leigh almost asked Harmony if she meant Dancing Dawn or her. But then she was being pushed out of the box, her whole group acting as her escort to the winner's circle.

"Too bad your mama's not here," Jennifer said. "Dancing Dawn winning...and High Flyer's bound to take the Blue Grass Stakes," she said of the next race. "I can't believe she would miss this."

"Mama's under the weather. Said she'd rather watch the Stakes on television this time."

"That doesn't sound like Vanessa," Nolan said. "Nothing serious wrong, I hope."

Leigh hoped, as well. The thought put a cloud over the win. Mama had been acting awfully strange the past month or so. Overly emotional and at times a little...unbalanced.

She rushed to assure her friends, "I'm sure Mama will be fine."

"And so I am, Ashleigh, darlin'."

Vanessa Scott materialized as they reached the fence around the winner's circle. There could be no doubt that this was Leigh's mother. Except for eyes, a milk chocolate, she looked like a mature version of her only daughter. Dressed in a pale yellow suit, with a matching veiled hat perched in her upswept silver-streaked dark hair, she also appeared every inch the owner of a winning filly.

Warmth flowed through Leigh. Seeing Mama like this, looking her old self after the way she'd been acting lately... why, it was tonic to her very soul.

Leigh's smile was brilliant as she hooked her arm through her mother's. "Come on, Mama. Let's go kiss our filly and collect our purse."

JIMMY DIAZ HIT the jockeys' room with barely enough time to spare before the big stakes.

"Find yourself a filly to ride between races?" muttered Ned Searle.

Not about to confide in his valet, Jimmy let him think what he wanted. A man played around once when he wasn't supposed to, and nobody forgot. He started stripping.

"Your silks." Ned held out the yellow-and-purple jacket and helmet cover.

Jimmy took them with a grunt of thanks. At least keeping his own mouth shut would help safeguard his reputation. Recalling the unpleasant encounter he'd just had, he grew more and more steamed.

There'd better not be any rumors flying around!

His empty gut screamed at him. Doc Martin had said he had an ulcer and told him to keep it soothed with lots of good, bland food. As if he didn't want to. Part of the reason he had the ulcer to begin with was his weight. It was damned near impossible keeping between one-twelve and one-fourteen without heaving his cookies after every meal like some of the guys did. Still, he'd given up a lot for his career, had taken more chances than most.

Now this... this threat....

He snapped his silks shut over his complaining stomach and vowed he'd do whatever was necessary to keep from losing everything he'd worked so hard to get!

LEIGH STRODE ACROSS the backside of the track, intent on finding Harley Barnett. Everywhere she looked, employees were milling about, busy at work. But nowhere did she spot Wind Racer Farm's head trainer.

She moved along the shed rows where the thoroughbreds were stabled, exchanging greetings with the hotwalkers and exercise riders as easily as she did with her day's companions, whom she'd left behind in the paddock area.

A groom carrying tack fell in step with her. "Hey, Leigh, congrats."

"Thanks, but brag on Harley," Leigh told him. "He's the trainer, he gets the credit. Haven't seen him, have you?"

"Cain't say as I have."

"He must be with High Flyer. Later."

Leigh entered the shed row that housed the Wind Racer mounts, but no one, not even a groom, was in sight. She approached one of the stalls. The nameplate next to the opening read High Flyer. The big bay inside whinnied nervously and shied away from her approach.

Leigh frowned. "Something wrong?" Then she called out, "Harley, you around?"

No answer. She undid the stall webbing and entered, her focus the colt. He eyed her suspiciously. She crooned to him and moved closer, her brand-new yellow shoes squishing through the muck.

"What's the matter, Bad Boy?"

She'd helped deliver High Flyer because his dam had gone through a quick labor and hadn't chosen to wait for the vet. Hers had been the first human voice he'd heard as a foal, and she'd given him his nickname when he was three days old. Even then she'd known he was going to be a mischievous colt. But now he seemed downright scared. He was one of the few Wind Racer thoroughbreds she personally owned, and she knew him well. She found his nose, brought it up so she could get a good look at him. His eyes seemed a tad wild. He spoke to her in low whinnies but he didn't move away.

"That's it. Talk to me. Tell me all about it."

Whinnying again, he poked her shoulder with his nose, leaving greenish spittle on her silk dress.

"Don't think I'm fancy enough, huh? Want to decorate me?"

Her hands and voice were calming him. He moved closer. She smiled and rubbed her face against the soft velvet of his nose, feeling a wet smear along her cheek. When he tried to mouth her hat, she pulled away, laughing.

"That's more like my Bad Boy. You're just nervous, huh?"

She was so intent on the colt she didn't realize she wasn't alone until Harley Barnett thundered, "What in tarnation are you doing in here?" as if she didn't have a right.

Leigh tamped down her annoyance at the beefy, wheat-haired trainer with difficulty. Harley had resented her since she'd insisted on helping with High Flyer's training. He'd been downright hostile since learning that she intended to take over as the farm's general manager when Thane Perkins retired, come the end of the racing season. She knew he didn't like the idea of a woman riding herd over him. In his early fifties, he was a chauvinist and proud of it.

She took a deep breath, disregarded Harley's reddened complexion and threatening snarl and calmly took control. "The question is—where have you been? Dancing Dawn won, and you were nowhere to be found."

"I had something important to do." What, he didn't say.

Leigh thought of demanding an answer, but keeping as much peace as he would allow seemed the wiser course at the moment. Besides, Micah Finley arrived just then to break the tension.

"Got that wrap you asked for," the wizened groom told Harley. "Though Can He Prance don't seem to be limping. At least, not now." He nodded to Leigh. "Time to let High Flyer strut his stuff, huh?"

"It's time," Harley agreed. He stared at Leigh as if she were in the way and ought to know better.

"I'll be getting to the paddock area, then," she said, still stroking the colt.

She was in no hurry to accommodate the disagreeable trainer. She'd spoken to her mother about him more than once, suggested that maybe they should look for someone else, someone who would feel comfortable working with her. Mama had been adamant about keeping Harley. Said she wouldn't hear of his being replaced. Leigh guessed she could understand her mother's position, considering Harley had been with the farm near forever—since before her father died.

She ruffled the colt's mane. "You go out there and do your best for Wind Racer Farm, you hear me, Bad Boy?"

High Flyer whinnied and turned his back to her. Leigh shook her head in puzzlement. She took her own sweet time leaving the stall, while Harley practically ground his teeth in frustration. The colt really was acting peculiar, and Harley wasn't commenting—not that she had doubts the trainer would do what was best for High Flyer.

Looking down at her new yellow shoes, she realized they were caked with muck. That would never do. At the end of their shed row, she walked around to the side, hoping to find a rag near the faucet. No luck. She hated the idea of running water over the fine leather and possibly ruining it. She'd counted on these heels to carry her through the season. While she did her best to keep up appearances, she couldn't afford to be extravagant.

Rounding the building, she found an old sponge out back, and as she returned to the faucet area, a movement caught her eye. A wheelchair disappeared on the other side of the next shed row, which belonged to Wingate Stud, her ex-husband's farm.

Leigh heard a woman's strained voice—"Daddy, what are you doin' back here?"—but couldn't make out Claude Walker's answer.

Shaking her head, Leigh concentrated on cleaning her shoes. Claude's racing accident had been a real tragedy. The famous jockey had been cut down in his prime, confined to a wheelchair for the rest of his life.

When she was satisfied with the condition of her shoes, Leigh headed for the paddock, only to have Desiree Walker fall in step with her. The jockey's flyaway blond hair was braided and tied together in the back and for the race would be tucked up under the helmet she was carrying.

"So, how do you feel about my riding for your husband and against you?"

Leigh glanced at the familiar black-and-gold silks. "Though he might have you think otherwise, Keith is my *ex*-husband." She smiled at the smaller woman who had been first a childhood friend, then a jockey they'd often hired to ride Wind Racer mounts in the past until Keith had made her better offers as part of his economic war against Leigh. "And I don't feel anything about it except disappointment that you're going to get beat."

Desiree grinned up at her. "Fat chance. Besides, who says I don't have the best horse?"

Everyone knew her daddy's accident had fueled Desiree's hunger for a career that would outshine his. One of the top-money jockeys at Keeneland and Churchill Downs in Kentucky and Gulfstream in Florida, the tiny woman had a reputation for being ruthless. Some said she'd ride right over a competitor to win a race. Then again, Desiree was an easy target in a patriarchal sport. If she were a man, she would be considered just plain tough. And good.

Leigh could relate to the inequity.

"So you really think Typhoon's faster than High Flyer?" she asked the jockey.

So far, the colts had only raced against each other twice before as two-year-olds. Each had one win and one place to the other. This would be the first time they met head-on as three-year-olds.

"Today will tell, won't it?" Desiree said. "One of them will make their granddaddy proud." Their "granddaddy" being Fly Like the Wind, the Kentucky Derby winner that had made Wind Racer Farm famous twenty years before. "I'm ready to do everything I can to bring Typhoon in for a win."

The women separated at the paddock, Desiree going to Keith for last-minute instructions on her ride. Leigh found her mother and stayed as far away from her ex-husband as the small area inside the walking ring would allow. With his pretty-boy, gold-and-tan *GQ* look, he got enough attention as it was. He always had. That had been the problem between them, because he hadn't kept his admirers at bay. The stallions hadn't been the only studs getting action behind the barns.

When Micah led High Flyer in, Leigh watched carefully. The normally outgoing colt shied from the spectators lining the walking ring, giving Micah a start.

"Do you think he'll be all right?" she asked her mother in a low tone. "He seems awfully nervous, don't you think?"

Vanessa Scott paled, and Leigh didn't know whether to be more concerned about the colt or her mother.

"I'm certain he'll be fine once he gets to the track," Vanessa said, sounding as though she was trying to convince herself.

High Flyer was tossing his head and backing up. Worry wormed inside Leigh, even though the colt's manner wasn't extreme. It was just...unexpected. Something told her they were in for trouble.

"He's a little jittery today," she heard Harley tell Jimmy Diaz while giving the jockey a leg up. "Real unusual. Keep extra-alert."

Leigh didn't like that. Nor did she like the jockey's reaction. She swore she noted a wildness in Jimmy's eyes and a fine tremor in his hands. But what to do? You didn't scratch a horse from a race unless he was hurt or a possible danger out on the track. Harley hadn't declared him either, and he was the trainer. He'd be impossible to work with if she made such a decision without him, based on a hunch.

When the jockeys rode their mounts out, Leigh hooked arms with her mother and made for their box. All she could do was hope that her instincts were wrong and hold her breath until the race was over.

DOYLE WATCHED in puzzlement as High Flyer fought being loaded into the starting gate with the same kind of stubbornness usually displayed by Typhoon, who was known for his mean streak. ''Wonder what High Flyer's problem is today. Never saw him do that before.'' Whereas Typhoon was always excitable and mean-tempered around the starting gate, High Flyer was usually calm and collected. And Jimmy Diaz wasn't getting him to settle down, either.

He looked to his father for an answer, but Oakes McCoy watched in tight-lipped silence. Okay, so his father was in a weird mood today, too. A lifer in the thoroughbred racing industry, for years having been head groom over at Wingate Stud, Oakes usually had an opinion on anything and everything connected to his only passion in life.

But Doyle didn't have time to question his father as the race started.

''And they're off!'' Oakes muttered.

Even though he'd get to watch the replay of the race as many times as he wanted, Doyle quickly jotted notes of his first impressions in shorthand. What a race, considering the two Blue Grass Stakes favorites were the equine equivalents of first cousins! One of whom was his father's charge, Doyle reminded himself—he ought to be rooting for Typhoon.

Scandal took the lead with False Pretenses hot on his tail. Then came Ruling Passion and Gray's Charade. Typhoon and High Flyer settled in right behind.

And right where they ought to be, Doyle thought. Neither colt would be asked for speed this early in the race.

Doyle knew Typhoon and High Flyer each had totaled three wins out of five starts in their first year of racing. And so far this season, each had won two out of two prep races for the Kentucky Derby.

False Pretenses edged out Scandal for the lead.

He had no doubts that both colts would be in the money. As accurate a handicapper as any around, he still had no way of predicting which horse had the edge, though in print he'd given Typhoon a sliver, because Desiree's record as a jockey was slightly better than Jimmy's.

"Gray's Charade is dropping back," Oakes said as the colts approached the second turn.

Now the real race began, Doyle thought. High Flyer looking for a spot at the rail...Typhoon getting an opening between Ruling Passion and Scandal...and down the stretch they came!

Staring intently, Doyle watched as the almost identical bay colts fired at precisely the same moment, High Flyer keeping to the rail, Typhoon surging between Ruling Passion and Scandal, while members of the audience surged to their feet and offered loud encouragement to whichever horses they bet on.

"High Flyer has the lead!" yelled a man behind Doyle. But Typhoon was only a nose behind. Ruling Passion dropped to third and was losing speed.

The entire crowd roared, with the possible exception of Oakes McCoy. The old man was gripping the rail, muttering to himself. And Doyle was certain he correctly heard his father utter the name "Jimmy."

Could the old man possibly be rooting for the competition instead of for his own employer's horse?

JIMMY USED THE CROP ONCE and felt High Flyer jump a little too sharply. What the hell was wrong with the colt? Typhoon was breathing down his neck, edging closer and closer, squeezing into the periphery of Jimmy's tunnel vision.

No, damn it! He couldn't lose today!

He cropped the colt again and felt another nervous surge that sent him rocking in his stirrups. What the hell was wrong here?

The finish line. He could see it!

High Flyer and Typhoon . . . fighting . . . neck and neck. The names yelled by the crowd echoed after Jimmy, and he knew it would be a dead heat all the way to the finish line.

Couldn't lose. Not today. . . .

His hand swept back . . . High Flyer's ears flattened, head cocked . . . Typhoon closer . . . colts nosing the finish line together . . . crop down and touching . . .

And then all hell broke loose.

Jimmy felt High Flyer go straight up and sideways, muscles surging to the left. "No!"

Jimmy let go as the colt jumped the rail. He flew a few feet and landed in the ditch on the other side with a sickening thud and crack. More broken bones.

Then the stunner . . . thirteen-hundred pounds of frantic horse coming for him in slow motion . . . the dark bulk blotting out the sky . . .

Jimmy couldn't move, could only pray.

Contact!

His breath was crushed out of him, and he experienced a searing, agonizing pain unlike any he'd felt before, and then . . . nothing.

Chapter Two

A horrified cry rose from the crowd as High Flyer's rear leg hooked onto the rail and the colt went tumbling down hard on the small man in yellow-and-purple silks.

Tears sprang to Leigh's eyes and a choked breath caught in her throat. High Flyer lay there, legs thrashing, unable to rise. She couldn't even see Jimmy Diaz buried beneath the heaving horseflesh.

"Oh, no. God, no!" Let Jimmy be okay. And the colt.

She'd sensed something terrible was going to happen. Why hadn't she acted on her instinct? There was always the chance of an accident at a race, even a possible tragedy, but still, how could she have envisioned *this?*

"Vanessa!" Nolan yelled, and a stunned Leigh turned in time to see Mama crumpling and him catching her.

Leigh helped Nolan sit her unconscious mother in a chair. She rubbed the slender, aristocratic hands that were as cold as ice, and spoke in a soft, soothing tone. "Mama, wake up now, hear? Mama?"

Vanessa's eyes fluttered open. At first she looked confused, as if wondering why she was the object of so much attention. Then her eyes cleared. She blinked a few times and went into a state of panic. Her body grew rigid and she began gasping for air.

"A doctor, please! Someone get a doctor!" Leigh implored. She prayed her mother wasn't having a heart attack on top of everything else.

"I'm a doctor."

In shock herself, Leigh backed off to give the stranger some room. Quickly checking Vanessa's vital signs, he ascertained she was merely having a severe stress reaction. He and Nolan half carried her off toward the first-aid station.

When Leigh started to follow, Jennifer said, "You'd better see to your horse and jockey."

Looking after her mother worriedly, Leigh knew Jennifer was right. Mama would be okay and she wasn't alone. Someone had to take responsibility on the field. She glanced down to the track. High Flyer was standing now, but she couldn't see Jimmy.

She rushed down to ground level as fast as the crowd would allow. Everything had stopped while the spectators waited for news of the fate of horse and jockey. People were speculating whether Jimmy would make it without any broken bones this time, and whether he mightn't be in a wheelchair like poor Claude Walker, who'd been crippled at this very track ten years before. Others were making bets on whether or not High Flyer would ever race again.

Leigh tried to shut out the voices, the horrid conjectures, but nightmares had a way of creeping into a person's very soul.

Taking the tunnel beneath the grandstand out to the track, she crossed the path of some horses coming in from the field. The jockeys were stone-faced. "Is Jimmy all right?" she asked one of them.

He shrugged and shook his head.

And Leigh flew the rest of the way through the tunnel.

"Ashleigh, honey, can I do anything?" came a concerned male voice at the other end.

Leigh slowed, realized her ex-husband was waiting for his purse in the winner's circle. Keith Wingate's features were set in a sympathetic expression that somehow played false. Behind him, a grim Oakes McCoy held on to a skittish Typhoon. And Desiree Walker was trying not to cry. Her shoulders shook with her swallowed sobs.

Guessing what the winning jockey was feeling, Leigh told him, "Take care of Desiree. Try convincing your jockey she's not to blame."

She sped across the track. Two ambulances had arrived, one for Jimmy, the other for High Flyer. The colt was limping, but Harley and the veterinarian easily walked him into the larger vehicle. Jimmy wasn't so lucky. He was tied down to a stretcher so that nothing would move, and the paramedics were hurrying to get him off the field, as if every second counted.

As they slid him into the ambulance, Leigh saw blood bubbling from his mouth and beneath his white silk breeches, both legs bent where there were no joints.

She went woozy and only held on to herself with determination.

"Is he going to be all right?" she asked one of the medics. When she got no answer, only a closed expression, she grew panicky. "He's going to live, isn't he?"

"If he does," came Harley's voice from behind her, "it'll be the worst thing that ever happened to him."

JIMMY DIAZ passed on just before dawn without ever waking. The waiting room was filled with people from the backside who wept at the news.

Leigh wept, too. Harley had been correct about the extent and severity of Jimmy's injuries. Both legs shattered, neck fractured, both lungs collapsed and punctured from broken ribs. She'd only considered death to be merciful once before—when her own father had been taken after a five-year bout with lung cancer.

"It's my fault," sobbed Desiree.

Either Keith hadn't found the right words to convince her otherwise or he hadn't even tried. More likely the latter, Leigh thought. Her ex-husband was a selfish bastard, and no doubt the win for Typhoon had been the only thing on his mind. Desiree had been crying off and on all night.

"It's no one's fault," she assured the other woman yet again. "It was a horrible accident. A tragedy. But no one's to blame." Except herself, maybe, for not acting when she'd sensed something was wrong.

"I shouldn't have let Typhoon get so close. He's so mean he spooks other horses all the time. But I never thought one would jump the rail."

Though they were aggressive competitors out on the track, off the track jockeys were a close-knit bunch because of shared experiences—especially the danger and injuries they all endured.

"No one could have guessed," Leigh said. It hadn't even occurred to *her.* "Listen, why don't I take you home where you can get some rest?"

"Thanks, Leigh. You're a good friend. I hate the thought of driving alone."

Leigh had been surprised that Claude Walker hadn't kept vigil with his daughter, considering how close they were and all. Desiree even lived with her daddy, had moved back home to his tiny farm near Midway after his accident. Leigh supposed that's why he hadn't come to the hospital. He woke every morning to live with the results of his own injuries—undoubtedly he hadn't been able to tolerate waiting to hear about Jimmy's.

As they crossed the waiting room to the exit, they came face-to-face with Doyle McCoy and his father. Oakes appeared ashen, rivulets of tears driving lines into his cheeks. And while Doyle wasn't crying openly, he looked like a man who had just lost his best friend. Not far from the truth. Leigh remembered he and Jimmy had been buddies all the way through high school.

"Doyle, I am truly sorry," Leigh said. She swiped at a tear that threatened to embarrass her. "I know you loved Jimmy...." Her words trailed off, and she coughed to smother a sob.

"Thank you, Ash—" Doyle started and then added the "—Leigh," with a note of respect he hadn't offered her in years.

Their eyes met without animosity for one single moment, and a yearning she'd suppressed forever ago came back to haunt her. Then he looked away, and the spell was broken.

Leigh led Desiree out to her car and took the grieving jockey home. She watched the small figure slip into the house like a ghost.

By the time Leigh arrived back at Wind Racer the sun was shining brightly, setting the fields of bluegrass ablaze. Too bad, she thought, the stunning color only lasted such a short time in spring, the special glow disappearing when the tiny blue blooms were mowed. The acreage was surrounded in part by old slave walls—horizontal gray stones topped by a layer of vertical stones—and four-board black fencing.

She remembered when they could afford to paint the fencing white before her daddy took ill. Almost no one could anymore, she knew. Most of the farms in the area were victims of tremendous change due to the ailing economy.

Leigh only wished such change wasn't happening to Wind Racer so fast. Turning into the long drive to the stately old house, she looked over the pastures where mares grazed with their foals cavorting around them. She would miss bringing foals into the world, taking care of these sweet horse babies and their mamas. She adored being brood manager of Wind Racer, but Thane Perkins was getting too old to deal with the constant stress of keeping the farm up-to-date on too little money.

The main reason Leigh couldn't see hiring a new general manager.

Things seemed to be getting worse and worse for the farm. Money had been real tight, especially so recently, maybe for the last six months. Mama wouldn't let her dig around in the finances yet, but that would change when she took over.

And she *would* take over, she thought as she parked and sat looking out over the precious land that was part of her very soul.

Leigh sighed. Becoming general manager of the farm was a natural step forward for her, considering she would own the whole business one day. Too bad the job would have its drawbacks—like working with Harley Barnett, a man who had no use for her. If the trainer stuck, that is. She'd heard rumors that he'd been putting out feelers, that he was thinking of making a go of it on his own if he found enough potential clients.

She swung out of the car. Maybe Harley's going would be the one change she could look forward to.

The house was quiet—she knew her mother had been sedated—and she quietly made her way to her suite of rooms in the east wing. Kicking off her heels and shucking her silk dress onto a chair, she climbed into bed still wearing her underwear.

But every time she closed her eyes she saw the tragedy play over again in slow motion. An accident, she reminded herself. It wasn't her fault. Not anyone's fault.

If only she hadn't gone to the backside before the race.

If only she hadn't seen High Flyer's unusual behavior in the paddock area.

If only she had done something about it!

That the colt she loved so well was merely bruised and would probably be fit enough to run in the Derby was little consolation. How could that knowledge assuage the guilt she felt over an innocent man's death?

HAVING FINALLY FALLEN INTO a fitful sleep, Leigh awoke several hours later to find her mother in the kitchen, dressed in an afternoon gown as if she were meeting some friends for tea. Leigh herself was dressed in jeans and a T-shirt.

"I'm making chicken salad for lunch," Vanessa announced.

On the island counter before her, several cooked chicken breasts lay on a cutting board, along with chopped eggs and several sticks of celery.

"How are you feeling, Mama?"

"As fine as I can be, considerin'." While her mother sounded calmer, she seemed a bit brittle.

Without asking, Leigh fetched a second cutting board and knife and began chopping the celery. They worked together in silence for a moment, but she could tell Mama wanted to talk about the accident.

"You heard about Jimmy?"

Her mother's hands paused over the cutting board. The knuckles of her knife-hand were white with tension. "Thane told me. I am truly sorry I was not there at the hospital with you when he departed."

"Mama, you were in no condition." Unless as a patient, Leigh thought, remembering how out of control her mother had been directly after the accident. A year ago, she would have reacted differently. She would have taken charge. Another change that troubled Leigh.

"It's an omen, Ashleigh. The accident...and Jimmy's passing..."

Leigh heard a car pull up the drive. "What kind of omen?"

Her mother tossed the chicken into a bowl and started on the eggs. "I've been doing a lot of thinking.... Maybe we ought to make a change, get out of the business before it goes under and drags us with it."

"What are you saying?" Leigh added the chopped celery to the chicken and opened the jar of mayonnaise. "You think we should stop racing?" A fairly normal reaction to such a tragedy, she supposed. Her mother would get over it once things settled down.

"I'm talking about the whole business."

Horrified, Leigh froze. "Mama, you can't mean you want to sell the farm?"

But Leigh never got the opportunity to find out exactly what her mother meant. The doorbell rang. Once upon a time they'd had a live-in housekeeper to announce visitors. Now they could barely afford to have a local woman come in twice a month to help them clean the huge old house.

Leigh wiped her hands on a towel and went to get the door herself.

It was Keith standing on the other side. His perfectly tanned handsome face was grave. "Ashleigh, honey, I came to give you my condolences—"

"You could have done that at the hospital," she interrupted. "Oh, no. Pardon me. I forgot you weren't there with the rest of us."

He didn't seem to notice her sarcasm. "This isn't about Jimmy, although of course I'm saddened by his demise. Can I come in?"

Reluctantly, she stepped back and let him into the hall. He took full advantage and walked past her into the living room as if he owned it, which she knew he wished he did. Wind Racer Farm had been the only reason he'd married her. Of course, Wind Racer's best interests had been her reason, as well—not that it was the same thing.

"So what is it this time, Keith?"

He was handling a sculpture of a thoroughbred possessively. "I wanted you to know how sorry I am about High Flyer."

So he'd come around trying to find out how her colt was. "Why don't you just ask, Keith? High Flyer is bruised but he'll recover nicely."

"But he won't be running in the Derby."

"You wish. The vet said there was nothing seriously wrong, thank you very much for your concern. You may leave now. The door is this way." She held out her hand as if she needed to show him.

Keith didn't budge. He was staring at her with a wolfish grin that made her scalp prickle. He was up to something, and she didn't like it.

"You haven't heard, have you?" he asked.

She shifted uneasily and was silent for a moment before taking him up on his challenge. "Heard what?"

"That High Flyer was also tested for drugs. The results were positive—he was shot up with heroin."

"What!" Leigh felt as if the very breath had been knocked clean out of her. Keith's intention, she was certain. Staring at him, she realized he hadn't finished.

He almost sounded sincere when he said, "What a shame that your trainer's license has been suspended."

DOYLE MCCOY DROVE UP Pisgah Pike, straight past the entrance to the gracious main house on Wind Racer. He hadn't been inside the place since he was a teenager, and in those days he hadn't felt comfortable stepping out of his social class. Now he could step where he wanted. He had the connections and the money. Not enough to run a spread like this, maybe, but he'd come a long way from being the groom's son.

But today he had a mission. He was heading for the opposite end of the property and the smaller house where Harley Barnett lived. Because of Doyle's backside connections, he'd quickly heard about the investigation over High Flyer's drugging and wanted to get a quote from the trainer himself to include in tomorrow's column.

A few minutes later, he'd traversed the length of the property, pulled up to one of the farm trucks and parked in front of the neat white house that was plenty spacious for a bachelor. About to approach the front door, he heard raised voices from around back and went to investigate.

"If you didn't administer the drug, then who did?" Leigh was demanding.

"How the hell should I know?" Harley shouted.

"You sent Micah for bandages he said he didn't need and then you disappeared for a while yourself. Were you getting rid of the syringe?"

Harley swore loudly. "And I found *you* alone inside the colt's stall," he returned. "Maybe you administered the drug yourself."

"That's ridiculous!" Leigh sounded shocked at the accusation.

And she looked not only fit to be tied, but more beautiful than usual, Doyle thought, stopping several yards from where owner and trainer stood. It occurred to him that he might be intruding and that he should retreat and give them the privacy they had so obviously thought they already had.

He didn't move an inch.

"Yeah, ridiculous is a good way of putting it," Harley was saying. "But you figure it makes sense that I would do something so stupid, right? For the first time in my career I get a colt who has a shot at the Derby and I'm gonna screw up my chances by drugging him."

The trainer was making sense, Doyle thought. In all sanctioned races, the saliva and urine of the winner was tested for drugs. If an illegal substance was found, the winning mount was disqualified and the trainer suspended. A man could work his whole life and never get a shot at the Kentucky Derby. So why would Harley jeopardize his chances at the most prestigious race in the United States by shooting up his mount?

Heroin had been nicknamed "horse" because it had been frequently used to juice up race horses before strict testing procedures were established by the governing bodies of all tracks. Now less ethical trainers and owners were finding new drugs that weren't so easily detected. Doyle hadn't heard of anyone using heroin at a track in years.

"All right, let's suppose neither you nor I did it," Leigh was reluctantly saying.

At that moment, Harley spotted Doyle. Already dark with rage, the trainer's face grew rigid.

"Then, who?" Leigh asked.

"Maybe your friend Doyle wants to take a guess."

"What?" She whipped around, her expression horrified when she saw him. "Doyle McCoy, what do you think you're doing, sneaking around, listening to other people's conversations like some kind of pervert?"

He couldn't believe she'd lost it in front of him. Until now, the barbs Leigh invariably aimed at him had always been sugarcoated.

"I'm a reporter, remember?"

"Only in the loosest definition of the term."

She stalked him regally, looking every bit the outraged belle despite the jeans and T-shirt that were her work clothes. He had to admit the garments looked as good on her as had the silk dress.

"So, now what?" she demanded, looking ready for a fight. "Are you planning on getting some mileage out of recounting Harley's and my little disagreement?"

"Little?" Angry that she thought so little of him when he'd never given her reason, Doyle let her sweat for a moment. Then he said, "I plan on quoting Harley as saying he didn't have anything to do with the drugging. If you'd like, I'll include your statement, as well."

"I have nothing to say to you on the matter."

"Shall I quote that?"

"Doyle . . . please."

Doyle couldn't resist the vulnerable expression in her brilliant bluegrass eyes. He knew how much she must hate asking him for anything. He took a deep breath and let his temper simmer. "All right," he said agreeably, "why don't we all be civil to each other. I'm not trying to hang anyone in print. At least, not anyone who is innocent."

Leigh's throat worked and she forced out a sincere-sounding "Thank you."

"Apology accepted." Before she could deny her gratitude was equivalent to an apology, he went on. "Now, if neither of you drugged the colt to make him win—and I was not assuming that you had—then there must have been some darker motive at hand."

"You mean someone wanted to hurt High Flyer," Harley said.

"Or Jimmy." And Doyle would give anything to help catch the bastard who had ended his friend's life.

"You think someone actually planned to hurt Jimmy rather than the colt?" Leigh asked.

"Whoever investigates is going to have to consider all motives."

Leigh scowled. "What motives exactly?"

Doyle locked gazes with her. "How about murder?"

Chapter Three

"Murder?" Leigh's eyes rounded in amazement. "Jimmy? I don't believe it." Never would she have come up with such a wild conjecture.

"Even if the plan hadn't been to murder anyone, Jimmy did die," Doyle reminded her, "and the authorities will be required to investigate, though God knows whose jurisdiction this will be. No matter the motive, whoever gave the colt the drugs will have to be held accountable for Jimmy's death."

All the color drained from Harley's face, and he muttered to himself. "Son of a bitch. If the drugging charges stick, I'll be in one hell of a mess, won't I?"

"Then we're going to have to prove you didn't do it," Leigh said.

Harley gave her a skeptical look. "Yeah, sure."

"I'm serious." Leigh's mind was all in a jumble and she paced to walk off her sudden burst of nerves. "I have as much at stake as you do. Maybe not quite as much, but a lot. The reputation of Wind Racer Farm is no small thing."

In these harsh economic times, censure by the racing commission could mean financial and professional disaster for the Scotts. They might be frozen out of the business. The thought triggered Leigh's memory—her mother had mentioned getting out of the business that very morning. How odd. Leigh would be certain to quiz Mama about the unexpected turn of conversation as soon as she was stable enough.

"Sorry if I can't be as optimistic as you," Harley was saying. "And as far as investigating goes, I think I'd rather trust my life to the professionals."

With that he stalked off toward his house, leaving Leigh staring after him incredulously. Harley couldn't even be civil to her when she was offering to help him out of a mess that could destroy his life. He slammed the back door behind him as if in defiance of her.

"You can catch flies letting your mouth hang open like that."

"What?" She snapped her attention back to Doyle who stood mere inches from her, his rugged features pulled into a grimace that she guessed was supposed to pass for a smile. "You think this is a joke?"

The grimace disappeared. "I think what we have is a serious situation. Dead serious."

Leigh shivered at the reminder of Jimmy's fate. She could almost accept that the jockey had lost his life to a horrible accident—a tragedy, yes—but to murder? "I don't need Harley's approval to start asking around to see what I can find out."

"No, you surely don't."

The grimace threatened to return, and Leigh glared at Doyle. "You're making fun of me."

"I'm enjoying you," he countered.

"Well, don't."

"Why not?" Doyle kept his mouth in line. "I remember a time you practically begged me to."

"Ancient history." Leigh remembered, too—it seemed all she could think about back then had been his dark chestnut hair and hazel eyes and ruggedly handsome face that made her heart beat faster. She crossed her arms over her chest as if to prevent that from happening ever again. "Don't remind me."

Doyle was silent for a moment, and Leigh shifted uncomfortably under his gaze. She let her eyes drop to the nose that still edged a bit to the right and remembered how it had been broken.

Seventeen at the time, Doyle had stopped a fullgrown man from beating a yearling with a length of rubber hose. The jerk had then turned the hose on the teenager. Afterward, Doyle had come to Wind Racer to find his father, who'd worked for them as a groom. His face had been smeared with dried blood, his nose had been smashed beyond recognition. And he'd been determined to get Oakes to do something about the man—not for himself, but to make sure the yearling was safe.

Until that day, she'd been certain she hated the tough boy who treated her like a spoiled brat and made her nuts by calling her Ash. But on that very day, she'd fallen in love with Doyle McCoy. She hadn't told him so—had loved him in secret for nearly a year. And then when she'd finally opened her heart to him, he'd rejected it.

She had not taken rejection well.

Over the years, she'd turned giving him a hard time into an art form. Now she felt utterly prepubescent.

Why couldn't she think of a single thing to say to make him back off when she really needed to?

He was the one who broke the fine thread of tension stretching taut between them. "So where do you plan on starting your investigation?"

"Back at the track, I guess. Someone must have seen something."

"What makes you think anyone will talk to you?"

"Because I'm not anyone in authority," Leigh said. "I'm one of them."

Doyle's brows shot up. "Hardly. You're a Bluegrass blue blood—and an owner. You're not backside."

Leigh never consciously made that distinction. Yes, she was part owner of the farm, but she also worked with the horses. She saw the dams through their pregnancies, helped deliver their foals, then nurtured the babies on a day-to-day personal basis until after they were weaned and ready for training.

How could she be considered an outsider?

"So, what do you expect me to do?" she demanded, her temper rising. "Sit back and sip a tall glass of ice tea until the authorities come up with some answers?"

"That does sound like the sensible course."

He sounded noncommittal, but Leigh was certain that's exactly what he thought. "Well, I'm not going to."

She stalked away from him toward the farm truck she'd left in the drive but hadn't gone more than a half-dozen steps before his long legs caught up to hers.

"Maybe I oughta go with you."

"You're kidding."

"Backside people would take easier to me than they would you in this situation."

"Besides, you could use a good story, right, Mr. Big Nose Reporter? No thanks."

"I don't need your permission to come. It's a free country and I have my own car." When she didn't respond, he grabbed her arm and spun her around. "Look, I write a column about horses and handicapping. I'm not some investigative reporter who's looking for a hot tip. I promise I won't take unfair advantage of the situation."

"If you're not looking for a story, then why?"

"Isn't Jimmy a good enough reason?"

Leigh was ashamed that she hadn't realized why he wanted to be involved. Knowing his history, it only made sense that he'd want to help figure out why his friend had died.

She nodded. "All right, you can come along."

"Thanks so much for your permission."

And she chose to ignore his sarcasm.

In the end, she went along with him rather than he with her. After taking separate vehicles back to the main house, Doyle insisted they leave her truck instead of his car. Though he cited comfort as the main reason, Leigh was certain it was a control thing—he wasn't the type of man who asked a woman permission for anything. She went along with it because she wasn't in the mood to fight about something as silly as which vehicle to take.

Nor did she disagree when he suggested they stop for a quick lunch before heading out to the track. Keith's surprise appearance had thrown her off—she'd rushed right over to confront Harley—and she had never gotten any of Mama's chicken salad.

They stopped at the Crossing, a cozy restaurant in nearby Midway, a tiny town built around a railroad crossing. As was the case in many local eateries, the walls were decorated with horse memorabilia—framed photographs and newspaper clippings. And the place was filled with other horse people, many of whom either she or Doyle knew.

Over a club sandwich and ice tea, Leigh reluctantly got reacquainted with the man who had become a virtual stranger to her.

"You must put on a lot of mileage driving back and forth to your office every day."

The *Louisville Envoy* was about an hour's drive from Versailles, the town where he lived. In the middle of horse-farm country, Versailles was actually closer to Lexington than Louisville.

Doyle swallowed a mouthful of his burger and washed it down with a swig of Coca-Cola. "Who says I go in every day? Unless Churchill Downs is open, I rarely get to the office more than once a week."

"But your column—"

"Welcome to the wonderful world of FAX. I like living where a man can still take a breath of fresh air. I was never a big-city boy."

"Louisville a big city?" The thought made Leigh smile. "What do you do when you have to go into New York City to cover stakes races at Belmont?"

He gave her an exaggerated shudder. "The best I can."

They both laughed, but sobering thoughts about the tragedy quickly intruded.

"You and Jimmy," Leigh began. "Were you still as close as I remember?" As teenagers, she recalled, they'd been together nearly all the time.

"Not like when we were kids, no. We even lost touch for a few years," Doyle admitted. "After high school, I went off to college while Jimmy made the track circuit. But eventually our paths crossed again when I started covering thoroughbred racing. Whenever we happened to be in the same city, we'd go out for a couple of beers or dinner or whatever. And it always seemed as if time hadn't passed, as if we were still the same *compadres* we were as kids."

Remembering how his nose had been broken, Leigh wondered if a person with such a strong sense of moral conviction encompassing all God's creatures could really change deep down.

"Are you sure you're not the same Doyle McCoy I knew?" She wanted to bite her tongue when she almost added *and loved*.

"In some ways, I guess." He chuckled. "I don't want to be a jockey anymore, though."

She almost choked on her mouthful of turkey and bacon. "*You* wanted to be a jockey?"

"That was a long, long time ago remember."

"Tell me."

"Jimmy's old man was a jockey, you know."

"No, I didn't."

"So Jimmy started practicing on anything with four legs almost before he could walk. Eventually, he got me into it, too. For a couple of years there, we used to hire ourselves out as exercise riders. We'd take those horses out onto the farm tracks early every morning and dream about winning the Triple Crown. Then, just after my fifteenth birthday, my growth hormones kicked in. Jimmy's didn't.'' He held out his hands and glanced down at himself. "And the rest is history."

Leigh did remember him exercising the thoroughbreds on Wind Racer from time to time, only natural since his father had been a groom for them. But she'd figured he'd merely been looking for a way to make money—and to ride horses he might never otherwise even come near.

Looking at him now, she could hardly believe he'd ever entertained any notions of being a jockey—the largest jockey was only five-five or five-six and maybe one hundred and fifteen pounds soaking wet. Doyle was nearly six feet tall and as solidly built as they came. She could imagine him as a boxer or a wrestler. But a jockey?

"So tell me your oldest, deepest secret desire," Doyle demanded, turning the tables on her.

"To make Daddy's dream come true. I want the thoroughbred racing industry to consider Wind Racer one of the top farms not only in Kentucky but in the U.S."

"And there isn't anything you wouldn't do to make that happen, is there?"

She didn't like the way that sounded. Her mouthful of sandwich suddenly tasted like cardboard. It went down the same way. "Pardon me?"

"It's true, isn't it?"

"I work hard, yes," she said uneasily. "I make sacrifices, but—"

"Sacrifices including yourself," he interrupted, his disapproving tone making it perfectly clear what he thought of that idea. "Too bad Keith Wingate wasn't properly appreciative of what the two of you could have accomplished as a team. With your breeding and his money, your getting to the top was only a matter of time."

Leigh clenched her jaw and sat back. Why had she let down her guard with this man? She should have her head examined. He hadn't changed. He'd always been prejudiced against the farm and thoroughbred owners. Somehow he'd seen the individuals working on the backside as being a more noble and worthwhile group of people.

"I think we should get going."

He eyed her half-full plate and protested, "I'm not finished with my burger."

She felt like telling him to stuff the remaining portion in his big mouth—then he couldn't insult her again—but she merely smiled and said, "I know you are as anxious as I am to find out what really happened to Jimmy. We can't do that sitting here, now can we?"

His eyes narrowed. "Then by all means let's get a move on."

He'd done it now. Doyle figured he'd ticked Leigh off good. A mistake. They needed to cooperate, not politely try to one-up each other as they normally did. That was the problem—things had been going so smoothly between them. Maybe too smoothly. He'd been feeling an attraction he hadn't wanted to acknowledge and so the first chance he got, he made certain she didn't have the opportunity to notice.

This day had been one mistake after the other, Doyle mused, including his insisting on accompanying Leigh to Keeneland. Why he'd thought it a good idea he'd never know. Thank God it was only for an afternoon. They'd find out what they could, turn the information over to the authorities, and that would be that. Then they could go back to their respective corners and come out fighting when they met by chance.

They were both comfortable with that.

Silence stretched between them as they set off for the track. Leigh hummed to herself as they passed a field of mares and foals. Well, he didn't feel like humming, and he didn't feel like keeping his mouth shut, either.

"Supposing High Flyer was the target rather than Jimmy," Doyle said, interrupting Leigh's stirring rendition of "My Old Kentucky Home." "That would mean the attack was really against Wind Racer Farm."

"The thought had occurred to me," she said, sounding noncommittal.

"Have any enemies?"

"Rivals, yes. Enemies? Such a strong word. None that I know of."

She was staring out the window, choosing not to pay him any more mind than was polite, as if she could discourage him from making conversation. Too bad. He wasn't about to let her off the hook so easily.

"Let's go with rivals, then. How serious?"

"You know better than that, Doyle. We're all serious about winning."

"All right, then—anyone holding a grudge against you or your mother? That's somewhere between rival and enemy."

Leigh gave him a sharp look and fell silent again. The tension was so thick Doyle felt as though he could cut it with a hoof pick. He'd struck a nerve!

"Who?" he insisted.

"I'm not certain."

"Not certain. What does that mean? That you're not certain if someone *has* a grudge or you're not certain *who* it might be?" She didn't immediately answer, and Doyle started to get exasperated. "Has something else happened to make you suspicious of someone?"

"Not *some*thing. Several things. We don't even know for sure."

"Give me a clue here, would you?"

Reluctantly, she said, "A few weeks ago, some of the mares and their foals got loose from one of the pastures. We caught them wandering down the pike, and one of the foals came this close to being hit by a farm truck." She held out her thumb and forefinger barely an inch apart.

"Someone purposely let them out of the pasture?"

"We didn't think so at the time. Seemed more like a fluke—a couple of rotted fence boards finally giving way. We figured the mares made a break out of curiosity and the babies naturally followed."

He pulled the car onto the road that would take them to Keeneland's backside. "But something else must have happened to make you think it might not be an accident."

"Last week one of the stallions somehow got hold of some bad feed. We nearly lost him."

"And again you blamed it on carelessness?"

"That's what we *wanted* to believe, yes...until Keith told me about the drugging."

"What? You mean before Harley could tell you himself, your ex-husband called with the bad news?"

"Oh, no. That would be far too subtle."

Bitterness slipped into her tone—Doyle was certain she was unaware of it.

"Keith delivered the information in person so that he could savor my shock," Leigh went on. "He's never forgiven me for spoiling his plans for the farm with a divorce. He wants Wind Racer."

Doyle rolled that one over for a moment, finally saying, "Or maybe he wants to destroy it."

Leigh didn't even hesitate. "I wouldn't put it past him."

Their discussion of her ex-husband came to a halt as Doyle parked.

They split up and for the next hour or so individually questioned grooms and hot-walkers and other employees about what they might have seen the day before—if there had been anything at all unusual. Unfortunately, no one had anything suspect to relate.

"Hmm, and you thought your coming along would make the difference," Leigh said when they met back at the Wind Racer shed row.

She automatically moved to the box with High Flyer's metal nameplate. The stall was empty. Doyle knew the colt had been returned to the farm where he would recuperate.

"Think anyone looked for the syringe in here?" he asked, figuring if the authorities had gotten in the act yet, he and Leigh wouldn't find anything.

"Do you really think the guilty person would have been stupid enough to leave it behind?"

"We won't know unless we check, will we?"

Within minutes Doyle got a new appreciation for the old saying about looking for a needle in a haystack. That the bedding needed freshening made the task even more difficult and unpleasant. Leigh quickly found a shovel and used it to turn up the straw and muck and pile it in a corner.

Doyle watched, appreciating the fact that she hadn't handed the shovel over to him. He grudgingly admitted that she worked as deftly as anyone on the backside. Not that she had to know he thought so.

Setting down the shovel and leaning on the handle, Leigh said, "No syringe."

"So much for that idea." When she began redistributing the hay, he asked, "Why bother?"

"True. It'll get cleaned up later today."

She heaved the shovelful she still held into the corner. A tiny *ping* caught Doyle's attention. "What was that?"

Leigh set the shovel down against the stall's wall. "What?"

"I don't know. I thought I heard something metallic."

"A needle maybe?"

They moved as one, both getting on their hands and knees, checking every inch of the floor. Close quarters. Too close for Doyle's comfort. Despite himself,

Leigh distracted him. When her soft bottom backed up against his hip, he had to force down the strange sound that attacked his throat; he covered with a cough.

Leigh whipped around and glared at him suspiciously.

"Allergic to hay" was his excuse.

She swung her bottom away from him, anyway.

"See anything?" he asked a moment later.

"No. You?"

"I must have been hearing things."

But Doyle was reluctant to give up so easily. While Leigh bounded to her feet, he sat back on his haunches and gave the area one last careful look. His gaze swept every inch of the floor but discerned nothing. It was only when he turned toward Leigh that a minuscule glint caught his eye. He glanced back to the narrow ledge made by a cross brace. A tiny object, half-camouflaged by muck, rested there.

"Well, well." Doyle retrieved and cleaned off what turned out to be a tiny gold horseshoe. "Look what we have here."

Leigh squatted and took the horseshoe from him. With her fingertip, she poked at the little loop soldered to the middle of the curve. It was twisted open as if it had been ripped free from something.

"A good-luck charm. Might have broken free from a chain or a pin."

A superstitious lot, horse people embraced everything from traditional organized religion to new-age techniques in quest of good luck. Doyle himself carried a lucky money clip he'd bought with his first winnings on a race.

"Think this means anything?" he asked, taking the charm and examining it up close.

"Only that someone dropped it in here sometime yesterday after clean bedding was put down."

"Could this belong to Harley or Micah?"

"Harley says he believes in hard work, not luck, and Micah is a real religious man. I've never seen him with a lucky anything, either. That doesn't prove this couldn't have belonged to one of them, of course."

Doyle stuck the charm in his shirt pocket and rose. "We can make some discreet inquiries and see what we come up with."

The words were out of his mouth before he remembered his intentions to turn over anything they found to the authorities and call this personal investigation quits.

"I wonder if Keith has turned to carrying a good-luck charm," Leigh mused. "He didn't while we were married, but maybe when I left he figured he needed outside help to get what he wanted."

"I'll ask Pop."

Oakes had been working for Keith for nearly twelve years. As head groom of Wingate Stud, he was Keith's right-hand man.

"If anyone would know, he would," Leigh agreed.

They were leaving High Flyer's stall when they practically ran into Desiree Walker, who seemed startled to see them together. Her father, Claude, had been Doyle's father's good friend for many years. He couldn't say the same about himself and Desiree. He'd liked her okay as a kid, but as an adult, she was a little too hard-edged for his liking, no doubt due to the struggle she'd experienced as a woman jockey. The thoroughbred racing industry still was very much a good-ol'-boy network.

"What are you doing in the Wind Racer shed row?" Leigh asked.

"I saw you come in here," Desiree quickly explained. "I thought I'd take a minute to tell you how much I appreciated your staying with me last night and taking me home this morning."

"No big deal," Leigh said. "I would have stayed, anyway. I was glad for the friendly company. But aren't you afraid someone will tell Keith you're here with me again? You know he'll consider you disloyal."

"I couldn't care less what he thinks. It's not like he's my employer just because I pick up a few rides from him now and again."

Being a free agent, a jockey could ride for anyone. But Doyle knew she couldn't really be that casual about Keith Wingate's good opinion when he owned some of the best mounts Desiree rode.

"How are you doing?" Leigh was asking.

"Better. Keeping busy helps, but I wouldn't bet on me today if I were you."

"It'll get easier."

"I hope you're right. So, what are you doing here?" She included Doyle in her interested gaze.

Suspecting Leigh was about to tell all, he spoke up. "Leigh granted me an interview. Naturally I wanted to see High Flyer's stall."

"I thought you were a columnist, not an investigative reporter."

"True. But Jimmy was my friend. I want to know how he spent his last day."

Desiree frowned and looked away from him. She suddenly seemed edgy. "Uh, I'd better get going."

"What's wrong?" Leigh asked.

"Nothing. I just have to change my silks for my next race is all."

"No, something's bothering you."

Desiree flashed Doyle an uneasy look before telling Leigh, "Listen, maybe we'll talk later."

"Don't let me stop you from talking now," Doyle said. "You can say whatever you want to in front of me."

"You won't like it."

"So I won't like it."

Desiree's indecision lasted only a moment longer before she said, "Jimmy had a terrible argument with someone right before the Blue Grass Stakes. It was over behind the paddock. They were both heated, but talking in low voices. I didn't get close enough to hear what they were saying."

"Hear who?" Leigh asked. "Who was Jimmy arguing with?"

"You're not going to like this," Desiree muttered, her gaze locking with Doyle's.

He shifted uneasily, his stomach suddenly knotting. "Who?"

"Your father."

Chapter Four

Desiree was correct. Doyle *didn't* like her answer. So his father had fought with Jimmy shortly before the jockey's fatal race. So what was that supposed to prove? What sort of disagreement could have tied in with the accident? He couldn't fathom the two of them arguing over anything but the quality of horse-flesh....

"I'll talk to Pop about it, but I'm sure it doesn't mean anything." He hoped the sick feeling in his stomach wouldn't pay off.

"Right." Desiree backed away, looking anything but comfortable. "You wanted to know."

Leigh gave Doyle a troubled look. "Maybe we should wait until later to talk to Oakes."

"No—now."

"He's with Daddy," Desiree said. "Wingate Stud doesn't have a race until later this afternoon, so they're keeping company out back." She indicated the area behind the barn. "I have to go. I have a Calumet Farm mount in this next race, and my butt'll be in a sling if I'm not changed and prancing around that paddock in ten minutes."

"Thanks, Desiree," Leigh called after the jockey, who was already running.

Right, Doyle thought. Thanks for tensing him up... the way Pop had been directly before the Blue Grass Stakes. Doyle remembered his father's tight-lipped silence when he'd looked to the older man for an explanation for High Flyer's unusual state of nerves. Then he'd shrugged off the nonresponse and forgotten about it. But in retrospect, especially in light of the fight, he had to wonder if his father hadn't known that something illegal was going down.

"So let's find Pop."

A quiet Leigh followed him out of the Wind Racer shed row. And Doyle grew even more edgy. She usually had something to say about everything. Her silence was damning in and of itself. She must figure his father was somehow involved with Jimmy's death. His instinctive response was to lash out, to defend the man who had raised him alone, the man who had taught him everything he knew, had given him his love of thoroughbreds. But if she had any specific thoughts on the subject, she kept them to herself.

They rounded the barn and came upon the two men relaxing under a copse of trees. Pop had dragged out a folding chair, and Claude had attached a tray to the arm of his wheelchair. They were using the surface to play cards. Doyle stopped and stiffened when he realized they were laughing together as if they didn't have a care in the world, as if one of their own wasn't even now being prepared for burial.

Oakes McCoy sobered quick enough when he saw his son and Leigh. But Doyle could hardly miss the wariness in his father's eyes.

"Doyle and Ashleigh." Claude clucked. "Haven't seen you two running together since you were kids."

Was the ex-jockey's voice just a little strained? Doyle wondered. Or was he himself becoming more than a little paranoid?

"Claude." Leigh gave the man who had once ridden some of Wind Racer Farm's finest mounts a bright smile. "How's it going?"

"As well as can be expected after what happened to Jimmy yesterday."

Leigh's smile faded at the direct reminder.

"A real tragedy," Doyle agreed, focusing on his father, trying to see him not as a son, but as someone who didn't have a stake in what Oaks McCoy might or might not know. He looked old. Though he'd been silver-haired for years, the face so like his own seemed to have aged overnight. "Can we talk?"

"What's stopping you?"

"Alone?"

"Don't worry about me none, Oakes." Claude checked his watch. "Your boy looks like something's troubling him." He was stashing away the deck of cards and tray in a carrier attached to his wheelchair. "Besides, I gotta get my carcass outta here if I want to see my girl win this next race."

He was off in a shot, wheeling himself faster than a body could walk. For a moment, Doyle thought about asking Leigh to leave him alone with his father, too, but he figured she'd chew his ear good if he tried to get rid of her. She'd suspect he was trying to cover up something.

"So what's so all-fired important?" Oakes asked.

Leigh blurted, "It's about Jimmy," as if she could read Doyle's mind.

The worn face looked even older. "What about Jimmy? Have they set his burial—"

"It's not about the funeral, Pop." Doyle was certain he knew it, too. "It's about his death. More specifically, about something that happened yesterday. Did you two exchange words right before the Blue Grass Stakes?"

Oakes paled, and his eyes shifted away. "Who told you that?"

"Desiree," Leigh said.

The older man sighed and nodded. "Too much to expect our having a few words could go unnoticed."

"Pop, what happened?"

"I got a note from Jimmy to meet him before the race. I went and he was already waiting for me. Real steamed he was. Never seen him so fired up. He wanted to know what was wrong with me that I was making such accusations against him. I didn't have the faintest idea of what he was talking about. Told him I was there because he asked me."

Doyle frowned, but the knot tying up his gut loosened. "So what was going on?"

"He had a note, too, supposedly from me, accusing him of taking a bribe to throw the race. I told him I didn't send any note and that I wouldn't dream he'd do anything but his best out on the track. I got him to believe me, I guess, but he was still shook good. We figured maybe someone was trying to pin something on him. Or maybe someone was just trying to make sure he wouldn't ride his race. We were going to pursue what and who afterward..."

"Only Jimmy died first," Leigh finished.

"That he did, poor guy."

"Pop, you told the cops about this, right?"

Oakes shook his head. "I didn't want to ruin Jimmy's reputation with such garbage. Bad enough what happened to him. Didn't want anyone thinking the worst now that he's gone over."

"But the authorities ought to know," Leigh murmured.

Doyle cut off further thought in that direction. "Eventually, yes. When we have something more concrete. No need to shed suspicion where none's due." Especially not on his father.

Leigh opened her mouth as if she were going to argue with him. Then she looked to Oakes, and her expression softened. She nodded. "I suppose the information can wait awhile longer. Just hope they don't question Desiree."

"She won't backstab her own to outsiders," Oakes said with certainty.

Doyle wasn't so sure, but he was hopeful that the jockey could be discreet for a few days, at least. "Do you still have the note that you thought Jimmy sent you?"

His father dug through his jacket pockets. "Nope." Then frowned. "Wait a minute. I wasn't wearing this yesterday."

Oakes headed straight for the Wingate Stud shed row, at the end of which was a small all-purpose office. As head groom, he shared the space with owner-trainer Keith Wingate. Doyle followed his father inside the near-barren room with its single desk and filing cabinet, three chairs and a coat tree that was stuck in one corner. As if reluctant to set foot in the room, Leigh hung back at the doorway. Doyle supposed she'd been inside plenty of times while married to Mr. *GQ*. Probably held bad memories for her.

Oakes approached the overburdened coat tree. "It's in this one," Oakes said, searching the pockets of a jacket almost identical to, if cleaner than, the one he was wearing. But all he pulled out was some used tissue and a foil chewing-gum wrapper. "I don't understand. I know I was wearing this yesterday."

Even so, he spent the better part of five minutes searching every pocket of every jacket and vest hanging on the stand. And with each passing minute, the knot in Doyle's gut retied itself, tighter and tighter.

"What about the desk?" he asked his father, looking over the mess of folders and loose papers on top. "Could you have thrown it there?"

The older man obliged by searching not only the flat surface but every drawer of the desk. Finally, he gave up, plunked himself down in a chair and stared up at Doyle with something akin to panic in his eyes.

"Got me, son. I don't know what I did with it . . . unless I brought it home."

Doyle exchanged a look with Leigh, who kept her expression carefully blank. "Okay, Pop, take it easy.

It'll probably turn up when you're least expecting to find it. So what did this note look like?"

"It was a piece of paper, for God's sake!"

"What kind of paper?" Leigh asked, finally entering the room. "Something with the Keeneland logo?"

"Nah. Plain. Good stuff, though."

"Stationery," she said. "What color?"

"How the hell am I supposed to remember that?" He swiped a hand through his silver hair. "Kinda dark beige, I think. And the paper was thick and rough to the touch."

"Textured," Leigh added. "Beige textured stationery. That's a start."

"Yeah, terrific start. Now all we have to do is find the several hundred people in the area using stuff that fits that description." Doyle shook his head. If the investigating authorities found out about the argument and Pop couldn't produce the proof that this encounter was set up... He clapped his father on the shoulder. "You remember where you stashed it, you let us know right away, okay?"

Oakes nodded and Doyle began to leave.

Leigh gave him an annoyed look before asking his father, "Are you all right?" She sounded genuinely concerned.

"Yeah. Just trying to take in what an old forgetful fool I've become."

"You're upset, not senile," she said, bringing a half-cocked smile to the older man's lips.

A minute later they left Oakes to his work—he had to see to the next Wingate Stud horse to race—and crossed over to the Wind Racer Farm shed row, though they didn't immediately pile into Doyle's car. He leaned on the fender while Leigh paced the area between it and the long, low building.

His mind was spinning and he needed to air a few things with her. "I think someone's setting up Pop."

She didn't appear surprised, yet she asked, "What makes you so certain?"

"*Someone* sent him and Jimmy those notes."

"Mmm."

He could hear the question in her noncommittal response. "Or don't you believe him?"

"I don't *dis*believe him."

"That's not the same."

"I suppose not. I can't help it, Doyle. He works for Keith.... I just don't know what to think."

"If he was one of yours, you could."

"One of—"

"If he was some Bluegrass bigwig, then you'd be eager to prove his claims."

Leigh whirled to face him, her thick tail of hair settling over her shoulder. "Yes, of course I would. And I distrust your father on principle. After all, I'm narrow-minded and have no respect for the hardworking people on the backstretch. Why, if I could, I would grind them all under my heel—" she demonstrated "—into the mud."

Her sarcastic tone popped Doyle's temper. "Maybe you don't think about the differences consciously, but they're there, Leigh. That sort of prejudice is an inbred part of you just like in the other owners with histories in the thoroughbred industry."

She wasn't listening to him. She was staring down at the ground—at the booted foot that had slid in the mud. He watched her stoop and take a better look. Then her hand shot out, and she plucked at something half-buried in the muck.

"You're not even interested enough to listen!" Doyle complained.

Leigh didn't bother to disagree as she straightened. She was too busy unfolding a filthy piece of paper that had been crumpled into a ball. As the inside revealed itself, Doyle noted the color. Wheat—or a kind of dark beige. His pulse roared to life.

"What the hell is that?"

Eyes scanning its contents, she said, "A threat," and handed it to him.

Doyle frowned down at the typed missive:

Jimmy—
The grapevine says you're ready to let High Flyer lose for the right price. If you don't want this information shared with the racing commission, meet me behind the paddock stalls before the Blue Grass Stakes.

Oakes

Doyle read and reread the message several times. Rolled the wording over in his head. He for sure didn't want the cops getting their hands on this any sooner than necessary. A body could conjure more than one meaning into the threat.

Depending on one's point of view, it could sound like Pop was trying to stop Jimmy from throwing the race ... or that he was trying to bribe the jockey himself.

LEIGH BREATHED A SIGH of relief when Doyle pulled into the drive. Silence and a growing tension had ridden all the way home with them, and she needed a respite from his very presence. She couldn't hide her dismay when he removed his keys from the ignition and made to get out of the car as if he was fixing to stay.

"Listen, I have other things to do than play detective with you," she said, opening the door.

"I don't doubt it."

"The mares and foals are my responsibility."

"I understand perfectly."

"I have to make certain they get back into their barns safely for the night. And feed them."

"I'll help."

To her irritation, Leigh figured she wasn't about to talk Doyle out of it, so she swung out of the car and immediately stalked toward the larger field where she'd pastured the Wind Racer-owned horses. Being that it was dinnertime, rounding up the domesticated animals wasn't a difficult task. A few mares had already spotted her and were weaving across the field, every so often checking to make sure their foals were following.

The moment Doyle's long-legged stride caught him up to her, she asked, "So what's on your mind?"

"I thought we could discuss that over dinner."

"Dinner?"

"Don't look so shocked. We have to eat."

The last thing in the world she wanted was to have dinner with the crass handicapper. Look how lunch had turned out. "We already ate."

"Hours ago."

"What's wrong with eating on your own?"

"Then we couldn't discuss the situation and figure out what to do next."

In truth, Leigh was beginning to wonder if they *should* do anything more. Maybe they should never have started nosing around in the first place. She couldn't shake the doubt the threatening note had cast over Oakes McCoy and she was pretty certain that's exactly what Doyle had in mind for the evening. Shaking her up. He enjoyed making her uncomfortable.

"I think we'd better call it a day," she said, stopping at the pasture gate. "Maybe our getting in deeper personally—" *together* was what she meant "—isn't such a good idea."

"Would you be saying that if it looked like Vanessa rather than Pop who was somehow involved?"

He had her there. Her worry about Mama and the suggestion they get out of the business altogether surfaced in a rush. What if her mother *did* know something about the tragedy she wasn't telling? Not that Leigh could confront her about it directly, of course. Mama hadn't been herself in months, and Leigh feared pushing her over some invisible edge. No, she wouldn't chance making things worse if she could help it.

Leigh had to admit that if Doyle knew about their earlier conversation, he might have his doubts about her mother just as she had about his father. Not that she really thought Oakes was guilty of murder any

more than Mama was. Or even attempted bribery, for
that matter. She'd known and trusted Oakes McCoy all
her life, so why should she start distrusting him now?

"All right," she finally agreed, telling herself it was
for his father's and her mother's sakes rather than
Doyle's. "We'll talk over dinner. But that's as far as
I'm committing myself to this thing."

"Deal."

But she could tell from the gleam in Doyle's eyes that
he thought he'd won, that it was only a matter of some
sweet-talking to change her mind and suck her in good.
He'd soon find out he couldn't push her into something she didn't want to do! And she'd have to be crazy
to get any more involved with him than she had to.

One evening together, one shared dinner, and that
would be it, as far as she was concerned. Then he was
on his own.

"Let's get these mares and foals stabled for the night
so we can get going," Doyle said.

Giving him a look that merely made him snort, Leigh
swung open the pasture gate and let out a long, shrill
whistle.

The horses not yet at the fence came trotting across
the field. Normally Leigh had hired help to handle the
more than two dozen mares, but her assistant, Penny,
had the day off.

Doyle was as handy coaxing the mares out and over
to their barn as she was. He hadn't lost the finesse he'd
developed twenty years ago when, as a teenager, he'd
often helped his father around the place. He talked to
the mares in a low tone that should have thrilled them
right down to their not-so-dainty hooves.

Leigh knew that voice was working on *her,* stirring up old memories best left alone. She didn't want to be reminded of how crazy she'd been over him. The idea of spending time with him now made her uncomfortable. Not that she would let on, for she was certain he would enjoy the prospect far too much.

Doyle led a dam into her stall and held out a hand to the skittish filly who followed. The little chestnut gave him a suspicious look and a quick sniff before scampering inside the stall after her mama, whose belly was already swelling with one of next year's crop.

"What's the matter?" he asked, closing the stall door. "Don't trust me?"

Leigh chuckled. "Wise filly."

He gave her a look that threatened to melt her insides, and as he continued working happily, she reluctantly admitted she could almost see the young man she had once adored....

When they were done, Leigh closed the stall door and led the way outside. "Thanks for your help, Doyle. I'd be working well into dark if you hadn't volunteered."

"The pleasure was mine." He was grinning crookedly at her, and those hazel eyes shone with something she hadn't seen in them in years. "It brought back some mighty fine memories."

Their gazes locked, and for a brief moment Leigh felt a connection she wanted to deny. Remembering she had other things equally serious to take care of, she said, "I want to check on High Flyer before I shower and change. Pick a place, and I'll meet you."

"Hmm. Wouldn't be very gentlemanly of me to let you go on your own, now would it?"

"You mean you don't trust me to show."

He grinned. "That, too. If you don't mind, I'll wait. I haven't seen Vanessa for a while, anyway."

She couldn't help her immediate reaction. "As long as you don't intend to grill her about the accident."

"I promise that *I* won't bring up the subject. Not tonight."

Meaning he meant to grill Mama at another time. "I don't want you upsetting her." A vision of Mama passing out after the accident haunted Leigh. "Not today, not tomorrow or the next day, either." Never.

"We're all upset by what happened."

Steamed that she couldn't extract the promise from him, Leigh headed for High Flyer's barn, which was located near the practice track. The gravel road led up over a rise and then down into a deeper valley lush with blooming bluegrass. Fewer horses trod these grounds reserved for the stallions and the retirees. They passed a couple of small pastures where two of the farm's founding sires grazed.

"That's Fly Like the Wind, isn't it?" Doyle asked, as the bay with a white sock on his left foreleg looked up at them in interest.

"That's him. And the one in the next pasture over is Wind Tunnel."

"After all these years, they still look like mirror images of each other."

Leigh agreed. A white sock decorated Wind Tunnel's right foreleg rather than his left, but other than that they looked as alike as two horses could. Even the narrow blazes between their dark eyes were nearly identical.

"Being they're full brothers and all, their looking alike isn't all that unusual," Leigh said. "Some people mix up High Flyer and Typhoon—and they're only the equivalent of horse cousins."

Fly Like the Wind was the maternal granddaddy of both High Flyer and Wingate Stud's Typhoon. Now twenty-three, the Kentucky Derby winner was still the same good-natured, mischievous horse he'd been before he'd been gelded and put out to pasture. He'd lived in easy retirement for nearly twelve years now.

"Wind Tunnel still give you a hard time?" Doyle asked about the mirror image in the next pasture.

"He's mellowed a little, but not all that much."

While not as famous as his older brother, the twenty-year-old Wind Tunnel had won several Grade II and Grade III stakes races despite his difficult personality. A biter, he'd never liked close quarters, whether in the starting gate, during a race or while being introduced to a mare in heat. Thank goodness they didn't have to deal with that anymore. He'd been retired for a few years himself.

A loud whinny from the four-stall barn ahead told Leigh that High Flyer knew she was about. "We're expected," she said, relieved that the colt was alert enough to sense her presence. "I am, anyway."

"How do you know that's for you?" Doyle asked.

"Some males are quite fond of me."

But to her chagrin, upon entering the barn she found Micah in the process of feeding the colt, and she sensed Doyle's silent laughter at her. Leigh had no doubt High

Flyer had even more enthusiasm for his feed than he did for her. All four colts housed in the small barn were expressing their anxiety about their feed. One of them kicked a wall and let out a shriek loud enough to make Leigh wince.

"How's my Bad Boy doing?" she asked the groom over the noise.

Micah's gaze slipped from her to Doyle as he left High Flyer's stall, feed bucket empty. "Drug's worn off. He's alert. Still limping. Been treating his leg with an ice boot."

Patting the colt, Leigh stepped into the stall to check the leg decked out in a bright blue ice boot held together with Velcro fasteners. Despite Harley's claims that the injury was slight, she couldn't help worrying. The contusions that were visible would heal fast, but a thoroughbred's legs . . .

"He's gonna be fine," Micah said. "So wipe that worry off your pretty face."

Crunching his grain, High Flyer nickered and punched her shoulder with his nose as if in agreement. Leigh laughed and ran a hand up the bay's blaze to his forelock.

"You be good now, hear?" she murmured softly. "I don't want any more bad things to happen to you."

High Flyer tossed his head and went back to his grain, and Leigh backed out of the stall, sliding the barred door closed. When she turned and saw Doyle was gazing at her intently, she became self-conscious. If she expected him to tease or to try to irritate her, she was disappointed. His expression seemed . . . appreciative.

Then Doyle flicked his gaze to Micah, who was preparing a bucket of grain for one of the other colts. "Did you see anything out of order at the barn yesterday? Any idea of who might be involved?"

The groom's complexion darkened. "Like I already told the TRPB field rep, I don't have a clue."

The Thoroughbred Racing Protective Bureau was kind of a special security force for racetracks. A field representative was present at every meet, but Leigh hadn't realized he would be in charge of the investigation when something went this dreadfully wrong.

"So the rep has already been here questioning you," she murmured. "On a Sunday. Didn't waste any time."

"Me. Harley. Even Thane, though he wasn't anywhere near the backside all day. Now he's probably questioning Miss Vanessa."

"Mama! He's questioning Mama?"

Once more seeing her mother fainting, Leigh panicked and whipped out of the barn, racing back the way they'd come. Her legs pumped faster than she knew they were capable of.

"Wait up!" Doyle demanded.

But she didn't slow until she hit the rise and had a clear view of the house and the unfamiliar dark sedan sitting in the driveway.

Chapter Five

Wondering about Leigh's frantic reaction to her mother's being questioned, Doyle stayed practically on her heels right into the house.

The moment she entered the hallway, Leigh gasped out, "Mama, I see we have company!" as if she didn't know who it was.

"In here." Vanessa's voice echoed from the large room to the left.

Doyle followed Leigh into what he'd always thought of as more of an old-fashioned parlor than a modern living room. While some of the accessories might have changed, the ambience hadn't. And the same over-stuffed Queen Anne couch and chairs that he remembered as a teenager still balanced before the fireplace on rickety-looking wooden legs.

"Ashleigh. And Doyle," Vanessa said, her brown eyes widening in surprise. "How nice to see you."

"It's been a while," Doyle agreed, immediately understanding Leigh's reason for concern.

The woman who'd always been so vibrant now seemed a shell of her former self, as if only part of her were present, and that part delicate. Her complexion was a little too pale, her smile a little too brittle, her hands a little too shaky as she finished pouring a glass of ice tea.

Vanessa nodded to the man to whom she handed the fine crystal. "This is Mr. Win Kenney. My daughter, Leigh, and a friend, Doyle McCoy."

"McCoy?" boomed Kenney. The voice went with the rest of him. Hearty and well-fed. "The handicapper? I read your column."

"Mr. Kenney is from the Thoroughbred Racing Protective Bureau," Vanessa explained. "He's investigating High Flyer's drugging."

"Mama doesn't know anything about what happened yesterday, Mr. Kenney."

Leigh's tone was sugary—as false as her welcoming smile, Doyle thought.

"I'm sure she doesn't. Not directly. But I need to interview her, anyway." The gray eyes behind the thick glasses narrowed on Leigh. "And you."

At least he didn't say *question* or *interrogate,* Doyle thought. But he might as well have, for if it were possible, Vanessa paled even more.

Leigh seemed to notice, as well. She stepped closer to her mother. "I'll be happy to cooperate, especially since I personally own High Flyer, although he's registered to Wind Racer Farm." She turned to her mother. "Mama, didn't you say something about your sick headache coming on earlier? You should be lying down."

"I am fine, Ashleigh, darlin', and leaving would be rude. Please sit. You, too, Doyle."

Since both chairs were occupied, they sat on the sofa, Leigh taking the side closer to her mother.

"Oh my, how rude of me," Vanessa went on. "We were just havin' some ice tea. Can I get you some, Doyle?"

"No, thanks."

"None for me, either," Leigh quickly added.

"Now, where were we?" Kenney grumbled looking down at his pad. His notes were on one knee, while his brimmed straw hat was balanced on the other. "Oh, yes, the people who work for you. You say you trust them all?"

"Of course I do," Vanessa answered. "I wouldn't allow them to work for me otherwise."

"So no one would take on the responsibility himself to give you some unconventional help at winning a race?"

"You mean harm, don't you?" Doyle interrupted. "If High Flyer had won the Blue Grass, the automatic testing would reveal heroin—unlike some of the newer, more easily disguised drugs unscrupulous owners or trainers might try."

Vanessa set down her glass; tea sloshed over the top. The hand that mopped the table with a napkin shook, making Doyle wonder what was eating at her. She was normally so poised. Then again, it had been a long time since he'd seen her. And judging by the way she looked, added to the way Leigh had raced to her rescue, he guessed she might not have been well in a while.

"Maybe someone drugged the wrong horse," she suggested, sounding hopeful.

Leigh grasped on to that. "I was just telling Doyle how people sometimes mix up High Flyer and Typhoon because they look so much alike. Maybe someone *did* make a mistake."

"In the wrong shed row?" Doyle asked. "Because when else could this mistake have happened? Once the horses are led over to the paddock, they're never left alone until well after the race."

Leigh flashed him a dark look.

Kenney cleared his throat meaningfully. "Mr. McCoy, I appreciate your knowledge of the sport, but this is *my* investigation."

"By all means, Mr. Kenney, do your job."

Antagonism immediately glowed from Kenney, whose complexion mottled and whose neck suddenly seemed to bulge over his bow tie. The room filled with tension. Vanessa plucked at her skirt, tiny little pinches that left the material creased. And Leigh looked all wound up, attention focused on her mother as if she were ready to throw herself in front of Vanessa to protect her if necessary.

"Maybe I should question *you* since you seem so interested in this case," Kenney challenged Doyle. "Mixing up horses and shed rows seems as unlikely as the colt being drugged with heroin to win. So what is your theory?"

"No theory," Doyle returned, trying to put the bogus note from his father to Jimmy out of mind. The field rep could make what he would of the message, and Doyle wasn't about to share it until he could prove his father's innocence. "Just a lot of questions."

"The state investigator will have a lot more questions. Maybe more serious ones than I do. Unless I come up with something concrete, he'll be on the job tomorrow, or the next day at the latest."

Then he would have to get busy to find some answers, Doyle thought. Someone other than Desiree might have witnessed the argument between Oakes and Jimmy. He knew that, if asked, Oakes would blurt out the truth. And without the second note to back him up...

Realizing he'd overlooked something, Doyle flew up from the couch. "I hate to cut this short, but I have to leave."

"What about dinner?" Leigh asked.

"I'll meet you at The Barn about eight-thirty."

"But—"

"I forgot all about sending off tomorrow's column to my editor," he lied, backing off before she could protest further. He winced when he noted the dark expression wreathing her beautiful face. "Vanessa. Mr. Kenney."

"Bye, Doyle."

"I'll be reading tomorrow's column with interest, McCoy."

"Eight-thirty," he repeated before showing himself out.

In reality, he'd already FAXed the next day's column, a tribute to Jimmy Diaz that he'd written in the wee hours of the morning after the jockey's death. Whether or not Jimmy had been involved in some deal that had ultimately been the finish of him, he'd been a good friend and a great jockey. He deserved a final accolade. But those he'd left behind also deserved something. The truth.

He was about to see if Jimmy would tell it—not that a dead man could talk. But his possessions might have something to say. While his family lived down in Florida where the jockey had joined them part of the year when riding at Gulfstream or Hialeah, he'd always kept a small house on a few acres off Old Frankfort Pike.

Jimmy had been the type of guy who'd trusted the world and especially his own luck. He'd never seen any reason to lock up his house. Doyle guessed that wouldn't have changed—not unless Jimmy had something to hide. If so, Doyle figured he'd find some way of getting in.

He turned off the pike at a long gravel drive that wound up and around a hill and shot out through a couple of small tobacco fields. When he'd passed the drying shed where the large flat leaves would be hung until the tobacco dried, he took the left fork. A moment later he was parking in front of the small house Jimmy had called home during the meets at Keeneland and Churchill Downs.

Thank God, he didn't have to worry about breaking in. Jimmy hadn't changed. The door was unlocked. The realization made him breathe easier. *Jimmy hadn't changed.* His house was open. He had nothing to hide. Not that Doyle was about to leave without double-checking.

The downstairs was all one room, with the kitchen off to the side making an L-shaped pattern. The living room was double-storied, and the loft rooms—a bedroom and an office—overlooked the atrium. Didn't take long to check the downstairs. Not much to look through. Jimmy kept the place pretty neat. Nothing pertaining to business.

He went up the narrow winding staircase that was just about big enough for a jockey to the loft area. The bedroom was equally neat. Jimmy had even made the bed before leaving for the track.

The office area was a different story. Stuff piled everywhere. Newspapers, magazines, books. Bills, receipts, canceled checks. Doyle quickly sorted through the mess around the desk and files. Nothing suspicious. Half the weight was lifted from his shoulders. As far as he could tell, Jimmy really was clean. Proving that his father was equally innocent of wrongdoing would remove the other half of the burden.

About to leave, Doyle spotted a big old-fashioned leather scrapbook on a chair by the window. Oddly enough, he thought he recognized it. Could it be the same one Jimmy had bought at the start of his career as a jockey nearly twenty years before? He picked up the scrapbook and flipped the cover open. Yep, the leather container swelled with thick, oversized, overlong black pages to which ancient faded photographs were secured by those little triangular catches you had to lick and press to the paper.

Doyle sat and cradled Jimmy's memories of half a lifetime, a sadness overwhelming him. This was all that was left of a friend. His hand brushed the worn leather, and he couldn't stop himself from riding back through the years....

He stared at scratchy bleached-out photographs he himself had taken on Jimmy's first day as a jockey. His little buddy had been lucky to pick up a ride for a single race, but he'd posed as proudly as any seasoned veteran in his silks and, of course, had shown off with his mount. He'd wanted to remember that day forever. He'd even gotten a kick out of the photo Doyle had taken of him as he'd crossed the finish line dead last. It was there in this book of his life.

Doyle remembered that day, and others, as well. He turned another page. Jimmy's first win. He chuckled at the shot someone had taken in the jockey's room. Half-dressed men surrounded Jimmy—jockeys in the process of changing silks for their next race. A T-shirted Claude Walker grinned at the camera while pouring a bottle of champagne over Jimmy's head. The picture had been taken years before Claude had his accident.

Doyle thumbed through the memories, and for a few moments he forgot about the reason he was there. Reality snapped back like a rubber band, though, when he came to a photograph of Jimmy on a Wind Racer colt. He recognized the mount since there weren't many colts a track would dub black as opposed to bay or dark brown. Tornado. A real whirlwind on the stakes circuit three years before. Though he'd rarely won, he'd always been on the board for some share of the purse.

This picture had been taken after a win—the Jim Beam Stakes. Vanessa stood on one side of the colt, smiling and healthy-looking, the way he remembered her. And on the other side Leigh and her then-husband, Keith Wingate, posed for the camera. Despite the win, Leigh didn't look too happy. Talk about body language, she stood poker-stiff and turned away from the man.

Doyle wondered if that had been one of the times Leigh had caught her husband playing the stud with some other filly behind the shed row before the race. He'd heard the stories...

Leigh!

With a start, Doyle checked his watch. Half past eight, the time he'd ordered her to meet him at The Barn. And it would take him nearly a half hour to get there. He flew up out of the chair, nearly dropping the scrapbook. Lord, she would have a double-duck fit for sure!

Letting the thick black pages slide back into place, Doyle caught sight of the photo taken in the jockeys' room after Jimmy's first win. The familiar grin shone through the stream of bubbly pouring down his face. On impulse, Doyle plucked the photo from the page and tossed the scrapbook back onto the chair where he'd found it. Not one for keeping mementos himself, Doyle didn't have many pictures of friends or family. He wasn't certain he had one of Jimmy. And this was how he wanted to remember him.

He hung on to the photo as he rushed down the narrow staircase, across the living room and into the dusk. He wouldn't have time to go home to change, so he grabbed a sports jacket he always kept in the back seat of his car, slipped it on and slid the photo into the pocket before driving away as if the demons of hell were after him.

Which she probably would be, he thought, imagining the reception Ashleigh Scott would give him when he finally showed.

WHAT THE HELL was Doyle up to? His car sped right past the thicket of trees and spun gravel as it hit the curve. His being at Jimmy's place had not been part of the plan. And what if he returned? Wouldn't hurt to wait awhile, just in case....

Besides, dusk cloaked the surroundings. A few minutes more and no one could see through the dark. No one could make an I.D.

The plan had to change. That was obvious. If Doyle had been inside, then he'd already seen what was there to see. Too late to plant the decoy. Doyle and Ashleigh were becoming a couple of biggety amateur detectives! The fistful of money stuffed in a jacket pocket rustled with each step taken toward the house. But now it was too late. Doyle could testify that the wad hadn't been there when he'd checked over the place.

So why go inside at all?

Because the door opened readily.

And Doyle had been carrying something when he'd left. What?

A cursory once-over gave no clues. No indication that anyone had searched the place. Maybe upstairs....

The office was messy but not turned upside down as might have been expected. Lots of paperwork covering the desk, lots of reading material spread around the room. And on a wing-chair seat, a scrapbook lay open.

A closer look revealed a page of snapshots... and a space where one had been removed.

Doyle had taken it, of that there was no doubt. But why? What had he seen in that photograph? Something that could help him unravel the truth?

Pray to God not, or else....

NURSING A GLASS OF WINE at the bar in The Barn, Leigh amused herself by imagining different ways in which she could make Doyle suffer. If he ever showed! She checked her watch. Twenty-two minutes late and counting. Why she'd decided to meet him as ordered in the first place she'd never know, especially at a restaurant that was basically a hangout for owners, breeders and trainers and their friends. She recognized almost every customer by sight if not by actual acquaintance.

Knowing how Doyle felt about what he called Bluegrass blue bloods, this just wasn't his sort of place, so what was his point?

"Why, Ashleigh, darlin', what a surprise," came a melodious and familiar voice from behind her.

Leigh turned to see Harmony clinging to Nolan's arm. She hadn't seen either of them since her mother had fainted after the race the day before. "Hi."

"Are you here alone?" Nolan asked.

"Waiting for someone."

"Well, I'll be," Harmony murmured. "A man."

Leigh glanced at a wall clock. Twenty-four minutes late. "Loosely defined." *Worm* was more like it.

"Oh-ho."

"What?" Leigh challenged.

"Nothing."

But Harmony innocently lifted her brows, indicating she thought it *was* something, indeed. Before Leigh could respond, the redhead's expression grew serious.

"Oh, Ashleigh, I should have called to see if your Mama was all right—"

"She's doing better than Jimmy Diaz," Leigh said lightly, remembering how upset Mama had been after Kenney had left. Of course she'd put up a good front, but Leigh knew her too well to be fooled.

Nolan broke into her thoughts. "We heard Jimmy will be waked in town tomorrow night. Then it seems he'll be shipped off to Florida for the burial."

Leigh shivered and rubbed the goose bumps from her arms. Must have been an angel flying past. Jimmy? "His family has lived in Florida for years."

"Makes sense, then, doesn't it." Nolan nodded to the hostess who approached, menus in hand. "Listen, looks like our booth is ready. Care to join us?"

"Thanks, but I'll stay right here." To think.

About Jimmy. About what Mama knew. About what conclusions Mr. Win Kenney must be coming to and would share with whomever the state sent to investigate. Mentally enumerating the possibilities, Leigh watched Nolan escort Harmony to a private booth modeled after a box stall—the whole place was decked out to look like a designer's version of a real barn. Maybe Doyle's leaving early had roused Kenney's suspicions. That would serve him right!

"That scowl for me, Ash?"

Speaking of the devil . . . She looked up into cautious hazel eyes, then very pointedly checked her watch. Twenty-seven minutes late.

She gave him a chilly insincere smile. "You have an *interesting* sense of timing, Doyle McCoy, whether leaving or arriving."

He grinned. "I do my best."

Leigh didn't think it was funny, but she held on to her temper. There were other ways of showing displeasure than getting into a shouting match.

"What in the world was so all-fired important that you left me hanging in the breeze to deal with Mr. Kenney?" she asked tightly.

"My column, like I told you."

And she still wasn't buying. He'd been up to something. Wanting to get under his skin the way he'd done to her, she gave him a critical once-over. His caramel-colored sports jacket topped the same shirt and jeans he'd been wearing earlier.

"Had you gone home, you would have changed into more seemly attire."

"Seemly? Something wrong with the way I look?"

Dressed the way he was, his chestnut hair rumpled, he looked rugged. All male. And very tempting. "If *you* don't mind, why should *I?*" she asked, deliberately dripping honey. She wouldn't give him the satisfaction of knowing what she really thought.

But her tone didn't daunt him. He slid onto a stool and leaned closer. "I like the way *you* look. Get all dressed up especially for me, did you?"

That she had would go to her grave with her. "I do so enjoy being appropriate."

Appropriate in this case being a very feminine white blouse with full sleeves and a slim charcoal-gray calf-length skirt slit halfway up to being embarrassing.

She'd even woven a silver ribbon through her French braid and clipped large silver-and-onyx disks onto her ears.

Doyle certainly was being properly appreciative. While giving her an exaggerated leer, he flagged the bartender over and ordered a beer for himself and another glass of wine for her. No sooner had the drinks been delivered and paid for than the hostess arrived and led them to their private "box stall." Leigh had been hoping for one of the more public tables. She was disconcerted at being trapped in such close quarters with Doyle.

And determined not to show it.

"So, in addition to FAXing your column to your editor—which seems to have taken you nearly an hour and a half and therefore doesn't say much about your technical prowess," she caustically pointed out, "did you have time to think about Jimmy?"

If Doyle was feeling any guilt at abandoning her, he certainly wasn't showing it. "Jimmy's death is all I did think about."

"And?"

"And we haven't learned enough for me to draw any conclusions."

"That's it, then." Leigh was inexplicably disappointed. Not that she knew what she'd expected. That he'd found a way to absolve her mother and the farm when she hadn't been able to? "Tomorrow we'll have to turn over the horseshoe charm and the note to...whom? Win Kenney? The racing commission? The local police?"

"I don't think so."

"You don't mean to keep on—"

"But I do. And with your help."

But she'd vowed this dinner would be it, that they would talk over what they knew and she would be done with the investigation.

And him.

That thought didn't please her the way it should have.

"Look, I've been going over and over the situation myself," she told him. "And one thing is clear. There's nothing simple about it. I started out thinking maybe we'd learn who drugged High Flyer. I just wanted to get Wind Racer off the hook. But then, after talking to Oakes and finding the note, I realized it was too complicated for us to handle."

"Is that it, Ash? Or are you afraid we might find the truth?"

Leigh sighed. That was half of the problem... Doyle himself being the other half. "How would you feel if we discovered your father was somehow involved?"

"The same way you would if it was your mother. Maybe I'm crazy, but I don't think either of them was responsible. But they're both being affected, anyway. And I think we have a better chance of learning the truth than all the Win Kenneys put together. So what do you say? Will you see this through to the end with me? Please?"

Leigh was torn. She'd convinced herself she wanted out, that she didn't want anything more to do with Doyle. But that was a lie. How many lies had she fooled herself with through the years? she wondered.

About being over Doyle the moment he'd rejected her. About being in love with Keith. About not caring what she had to put up with to restore Wind Racer Farm to its former glory.

Wasn't it time that she was honest with herself?

The waitress arrived, pad in hand, giving Leigh a moment to make her decision. Because they hadn't even opened their menus, both ordered the house specialty—grilled steaks and twice-baked potatoes. Both also asked for creamy garlic dressing on their salads.

So they wouldn't be tempted to get too close?

"Well, are you going to help me or not?" Doyle demanded the moment the young woman left to place their orders.

Leigh nodded. She wanted to know the truth, whatever it was, and not only about the drugging. "What next, then?"

"We need to talk to Harley."

"Why?" Leigh snapped. "So he can spit in my face again?" She was still furious over the way the trainer had treated her that morning.

"He'll have calmed down some by tomorrow. And he'll have had time to think about his situation. Maybe he'll even be appreciative that we're trying to help."

Having to deal with the unpleasant trainer practically made her vision blur. "You don't know Harley."

Doyle cleared his throat uncomfortably. "And we'll have to talk to your mother."

"I told you I don't want Mama upset!" Leigh reminded him.

"A little late to be worrying about that." And before she could add another protest, Doyle said, "Besides, don't you think Vanessa will feel a little better if she knows we're trying to find out the truth. And that we're on her side?"

Thinking about the way Doyle had been so protective of Oakes earlier, Leigh wondered. "Are you on Mama's side?"

"I can't remember a time when I didn't like and admire your mother, Ash. That hasn't changed."

"Stop calling me that ridiculous name."

"You didn't always think it was ridiculous."

Doyle's intense stare made her shift in her seat. She almost felt as she had when she was thirteen. Full of worms inside. "I wasn't always in my right mind."

"You were too young, you know. That's why I did my best to discourage you."

"What?" It sounded as if he'd done so with some regret.

"But you're not too young now. Five years difference in age isn't anything once you become legal. Of course, there still are other differences. . . ."

Aghast at the implication that he might be willing to accept her affection *now,* Leigh stared open-mouthed until the waitress arrived with their dinner salads and rolls. She'd never been happier to see anyone in her life. After they both dug in and attacked the food, Leigh figured it was time to get back to business.

"About tomorrow—"

"Tomorrow will take care of itself."

"You said you wanted to discuss what we've dug up."

"That'll wait. I'd rather discuss you."

"You know what you *need* to know about me," she said, spearing a lettuce leaf with her fork.

"But not everything I'd *like* to know."

The way he said it gave her a start. Leigh warned herself not to be fooled. Doyle enjoyed torturing her. Maybe this was just a new tactic. Swallowing her mouthful of salad, prepared to have her dinner ruined just as her lunch had been, Leigh prompted, "For example?" She was certain he was going to bring up her mistake in marrying Keith again.

"Do you ever have any fun?"

Not exactly what she'd been prepared for. "I enjoy my work."

"What else?"

"I go to the racetrack when the farm's horses are running."

"Non-work-related."

She looked at him blankly. "You mean, do I like watching old movies while eating homemade popcorn? Taking long walks in the rain? Sappy stuff?"

"Yeah, like that."

"I don't have the time."

"Maybe you should *make* the time. No hobbies?"

"I ride."

"Mmm. Horses again."

She guessed that qualified as being work-related, too. "What's this sudden curiosity about?"

"I was just wondering how obsessive you are about the farm."

"It's my life." Leigh had never known anything else, had never wanted anything else, not since she was a child. Her father's dreams for the farm had faded with his death, but she knew she could make them shine once more. And she resented Doyle's trying to make her feel dissatisfied. "What about you? Do you have a hobby?"

He shrugged. "I used to have a family. Spent a lot of time with my kids. I haven't managed to replace them yet."

Resentment vanished as Leigh's heart went out to him. At least children hadn't been involved in her fiasco of a marriage, thank goodness, or she never would have been able to break the connection with Keith. She didn't believe in keeping children from a father, no matter how much animosity might exist between a divorced couple.

"At least you get to see your children, right?" she asked.

"I did until their mother remarried and took them to live in Virginia." Doyle sounded bitter. "I have two weeks of vacation and two holidays of *her* choice per year to look forward to."

"Couldn't you work out a more equitable custody arrangement?"

"Not after Susan convinced the judge that I could be a negative influence on my own kids." He appeared almost hostile when he admitted, "She divorced me over what she considered a bad habit."

The first thing that came to Leigh's mind was drugs. But then, she'd had drugs on her mind all day because of what happened to High Flyer. Not believing it of Doyle, she asked, "What kind of habit?"

"I played the ponies too much for her peace of mind."

A gambler. Leigh knew she shouldn't be surprised—many handicappers fell prey to this hazard of the profession. It was difficult for her to pass judgment on gambling when she was part of a sport that survived only because of the money involved in betting. A day at the track was a form of recreation for most people, no more expensive than many other activities they might enjoy.

Not that she was unaware that some people had real problems with gambling and shouldn't go near a track. "Did you lose a lot?" she asked.

"I won more than I lost."

"But your wife still didn't like it."

"Susan insisted she felt like there was a two-edged sword hanging over her head all the time. I couldn't convince her it wasn't a problem."

He'd lost his family and he still couldn't admit it, Leigh realized. "If you couldn't stop, not even to save your marriage, then it is a problem."

"I *did* stop."

"When it was too late," she guessed.

Doyle shrugged. "I haven't placed a bet in nearly a year." And as the waitress arrived with their main courses, he added, "But enough said about hobbies."

Silence stretched between them as they ate, making Leigh realize Doyle was uncomfortable. He probably hadn't meant to reveal so much of himself. She wondered whether or not he'd sought professional help to quit gambling. Being a handicapper, tracks were his life. If he'd really been as hooked as he made it sound, his calling winners for others without being able to bet on them himself must be torture. Kind of like a recovering alcoholic tending bar night after night, seeing and smelling liquor without allowing himself to taste it.

Leigh wondered how she would have felt if she'd been in his wife's situation—if Keith had been hooked on betting rather than on women. To be truthful, she guessed she wouldn't have liked it much, either. Addictions of any sort were unhealthy and potentially injurious to a relationship.

Unbidden, an accusation Keith had once made came back to haunt her. He'd claimed she was so obsessed with Wind Racer Farm that she didn't make enough time for him and that's why he'd turned to other women. But that had merely been his excuse to do as he pleased, she told herself.

Suddenly Leigh realized she and Doyle weren't alone. As if thinking about her ex-husband had conjured him up, Keith Wingate stood at the opening of their booth, gaze hooded, expression unreadable.

Chapter Six

"Ashleigh, honey, good to see you're getting out." Keith's tone belied the friendly words. "And with such sterling company."

Leigh stiffened and set down her fork. "Who I have dinner with is none of your business."

Seeming to sense the intensity of her negative feelings for her ex-husband, Doyle reached across the table and clasped his hand over hers possessively. "But thanks for the interest, Wingate."

Keith ignored Doyle and locked gazes with her. "Jimmy's wake is tomorrow night. How about letting me escort you and Vanessa?"

Knowing this act of kindness was merely a ploy of some sort, Leigh sweetly returned, "How about getting lost?"

"I know how you hate those depressing events."

"That's why she's going with me," Doyle said. "So your concern is misplaced."

Keith's light brown eyes burned as they finally acknowledged Doyle. "Don't get your hopes up, McCoy. You don't have what it takes." Without waiting for a response, he spun around and strode away.

"Bastard," Leigh murmured, glad she'd just about finished her dinner, for Keith had taken her appetite with him.

Why she'd ever been fooled by his smooth, golden looks into thinking he was a decent human being with whom she could build an entire life, she didn't know.

Realizing Doyle was still holding her hand, acknowledging how good it felt, how right, Leigh grew doubly uncomfortable and pulled free from his grasp. To cover her nervous reaction, she picked up her water glass and took a long draft.

"Quite a coincidence, Keith's showing up here," Doyle said.

Leigh started and almost choked on the liquid. "You think he followed me?"

"Or found out where he could find you."

"Why would he bother?"

"Why did he come to the farm this morning?" he returned.

"Because he's sadistic."

"Or keeping careful track of your movements."

Leigh stared at him, at the nose that had been broken in a noble cause. "Trust me, he doesn't want me back." Doyle would have been a man worthy of her trust, an inner voice told her. "The farm, maybe, but not me."

"Maybe he's figured out a way to get it."

Though he didn't elaborate, Doyle's words echoed through her mind for the seemingly interminable time it took him to flag down the waitress and settle the bill. The conjecture followed her on the ride home. She was so exhausted she could hardly keep her eyes open as the purr of the motor lulled her. But on some level, her brain kept spinning. Wondering. Trying to put pieces together. Impossible. They didn't know enough to draw any conclusions.

But she did know one thing. "I want to talk to Mama myself."

She thought Doyle might object and was relieved when he said, "Tonight."

"All right, tonight."

But when she arrived home, her mother was nowhere in the house. Leigh told herself there was no reason to worry. Just because Mama hadn't said anything about going out tonight didn't mean something was wrong. She'd cooped herself up in the house too much lately. Maybe a friend had called and they'd made spur-of-the-moment plans.

The problem was, Leigh couldn't feature Mama going off to have a good time on the heels of Jimmy's death. She couldn't imagine her going off without even leaving a note.

Wandering into the living room and settling in to wait for her mother's return, Leigh picked up the latest copy of *The Blood-Horse* but could hardly focus on the words. She was so very, very tired. But she kept awake by forcing herself to read, checking her watch every few minutes.

Sometime after midnight, she gave over and allowed exhaustion to claim her.

THE NEXT MORNING, Doyle had a hell of a time concentrating on past performances of the horses that would race at Keeneland the following day. First thing, his editor had called to compliment him on the column devoted to Jimmy, but if he failed to make some intelligent predictions two days in a row, Doyle knew the old man would give him holy hell. That readers would complain didn't mean diddly squat. No matter how hard he tried to concentrate, numbers of wins, places and shows, total money earned, names of dams, sires, trainers and jockeys all seemed to run together and make no sense.

Because thoughts of Keith Wingate kept intruding.

Realizing he was behind schedule, Doyle gave up the pretense of writing and headed out to meet Leigh. He could only hope the day would hold some inspiration for his work.

But Wingate was still worrying him as he turned into the Wind Racer Farm entrance.

Though he kept telling himself the man's appearance at the restaurant might have been a coincidence, he didn't believe the explanation was that simple. He wondered if Kenney had grilled Leigh's ex-husband yet. As the owner of the winning colt, Wingate should be suspect.

Doyle pulled over near the broodmare barn where Leigh and another young woman were reversing the process he'd helped her complete the evening before. They were pasturing the dams and their foals for the day.

Catching sight of him as he alighted, Leigh waved and yelled, "Want to help?"

"You're doing a fine job," he shouted back. "I wouldn't want to distract you."

She gave him a searing look and returned, ''We're almost done.''

Making himself comfortable against the fence, he found he enjoyed watching *her*. Leigh was as graceful as any of the long-legged fillies she tended. And equally beautiful. Her skin was cast with a golden sheen, her eyes fought the bluegrass for brilliance and her hair waterfalled down her back as shiny and long and thick as any horse's tail. Of course, he didn't dare tell her any of this lest she laugh at him.

He sounded like a sap.

A sap who was falling in...

''Lust,'' he muttered to himself. ''That's all it could be.''

But he had to admit that spending one day with Leigh had altered his attitude about her. Rather than just another magnolia-cum-laude graduate, he saw a woman who worked hard and cared deeply about others. He'd known that about her once a long time ago. Why had he let the Southern-belle facade she wore with equal ease put him off for so many years? Doyle suspected it had something to do with her choice of husbands.

He didn't have long to wait before Leigh joined him, thumbs hooked in the pockets of her worn jeans. Doyle tried hard not to let his admiration show. It wouldn't do to let her have the upper hand.

''Penny can finish up,'' Leigh said. She sucked in her breath and let it out in a sigh. ''Okay. Let's get it over with. Harley's down at the practice track.''

On foot, they retraced the route of the day before.

''How did your talk go with Vanessa?''

Leigh winced. "It didn't. Mama wasn't home. I waited up for her for hours. Then I guess I fell asleep on the couch. I didn't want to wake her so early this morning. I promise I'll talk to her later."

They crested the rise in the road, and Doyle scanned the area beyond High Flyer's barn. Four people huddled together at the practice track.

"Looks like a missed opportunity."

Vanessa leaned against the rail as did farm manager Thane Perkins, trainer Harley Barnett and his assistant, Josh Quaid. Doyle knew Josh would be the trainer of record until Harley was cleared of the drugging, but that wasn't keeping Harley from clocking the workouts himself. Two young mounts competed in a mock race, and as the chestnut crossed the finish line, Harley let out a whoop and held up the stopwatch. Josh quickly made a notation in a spiral notebook, and the two conferred excitedly.

"Looks like Harley thinks we have another winner in Hot Wind."

Leigh's positive words were overshadowed by the strain in her voice, and Doyle knew a moment's regret. But they couldn't spare Vanessa any longer, and he was certain Leigh knew that deep inside, for she didn't try to compromise him.

And it was Vanessa who spotted them first. Her instinctive smile faded quickly, however. "Doyle, you know I always like seein' you," she said as they drew closer, "but two days in a row after you haven't been around the farm in years... I would say you have something important on your mind."

Relieved that he didn't have to figure out how to begin, Doyle said, "We have to talk—"

But Harley interrupted. "He's sticking his nose where it doesn't belong."

"He's here at *my* agreement," Leigh told the trainer, her tone firm.

"*I* didn't agree to have nothing to do with him!"

"Getting a little overanxious, aren't you, Harley?" Thane commented, his weathered old face puckering in a frown. "Why'n't you wait to see what the boy has on his mind before you go a-cursin' him."

"I don't have to—"

"Harley!" Vanessa stopped him short. "Stop acting ugly, please. Let's go sit—" she indicated a picnic table under a nearby tree "—and try to be civil."

Vanessa's tone was unnaturally harsh. Doyle had never heard her raise her voice to anyone. Obviously, Harley hadn't, either, for he was staring at his employer as though he'd never seen her before.

"Josh, you take over here," he told his assistant.

"Got it covered, Harley."

Resetting his billed cap more firmly over his wheat-colored hair, the trainer stalked over to the picnic table, the others following.

"A man usually bends with the years," Thane softly commented to Doyle as they brought up the rear. "I hate to think what he'll be like at my age."

The farm manager had slowed some, Doyle realized, and he had grown thin and stooped, but there was nothing wrong with his mind. Doyle only hoped retirement wouldn't be the end of him as it was for so many formerly active people who suddenly had nothing to do with their days. If Leigh were smart—for he was certain she, rather than Vanessa, would take over when Thane retired—she would use him on a consultant basis. The relationship would be good for both of them.

Leigh stood behind Vanessa, hands on the older woman's shoulders. Her eyes locked with his in a silent plea. Doyle didn't need to hear the words to know her concern was for her mother. Vanessa reached up and patted Leigh's hand, then covered her child's with her own in a show of solidarity.

Once everyone was settled, Thane and Harley opposite her, Vanessa asked, "Now, what's this all about, Doyle?"

Doyle stopped at the end of the table and gave the wood a quick drum of fingertips. "Leigh and I have been doing some investigating on our own."

She nodded. "About Jimmy."

"We were hoping to find out what happened before there were any terrible accusations."

Doyle noted Vanessa's knuckles whiten as her fingers tightened around Leigh's hand.

She asked, "What kind of accusations? Harley's already being wrongly held responsible for the drugging."

"But not for murder."

For a second, Doyle thought Vanessa might faint. Her eyes fluttered and her breath caught in her throat.

"No, dear God, not *that*," she whispered.

An odd response, certainly not one he expected, but then, Vanessa wasn't herself.

"Here we go again," Harley muttered. "Come up with a new tune, huh?"

"Kenney's not mentioned anything about murder," Vanessa said.

"That wouldn't be his responsibility." Doyle kept an eye on the trainer. "But like he said, the state boys will be on the case today or tomorrow. Who knows what facts—or what fabrications—they'll come up with."

Harley merely appeared disgusted. "Think this through, would you, McCoy? Why in the world would anyone think Jimmy was murdered? No one can predict what effect a drug will have on an animal. Actually, it *should* have given High Flyer the winning edge."

"Intent doesn't mean anything when you've got a wake to look forward to, now does it?" Doyle took a new tack. "I assume no one here thinks High Flyer was drugged so he would win the race."

"No, of course not," Vanessa agreed.

"But what if it was so the colt would *lose*."

"Who...?"

"Someone wants us to think it was Jimmy," Leigh told her mother.

"What?" Harley demanded. "You had a revelation?"

"Call it a missive." Doyle hadn't started out to tell anyone about the notes. But how were they supposed to learn anything by keeping *everything* to themselves? "Right before the Blue Grass Stakes, Jimmy got a message accusing him of being willing to throw the race for the right price."

Face flushing, Harley nearly exploded off the bench in anger. "Jimmy Diaz fixed the race!"

Vanessa insisted, "Jimmy would never do that."

"We don't think so, either, Mama," Leigh said. "But there is a note—I've seen it with my own eyes. I have it," she admitted.

"Who was this note from?" Thane asked.

Hoping no one would share this information with Kenney or the state boys until he got more answers, Doyle said, "Supposedly my father—he's the one who told us about it—but Pop said it was bogus. He got one, too, supposedly from Jimmy, asking for a meeting. You hear anything about the two of them having words back behind the paddock stalls before the race, that's what it was all about. They got into an argument before realizing someone was setting them up."

"Someone who meant to drug High Flyer, then place the blame on Jimmy?" Thane's thatch of white hair practically bristled. "But why? And who?"

"One person," Harley spat. "We don't need an investigation to know Keith Wingate is stirring up trouble again. Horses getting loose. Bad feed almost killing one of the stallions. Now a drugging. What next?"

"That was our guess, too," Leigh admitted. "But we can't be certain Keith was responsible."

"Bull!" Harley roared. "It's as plain as the nose on your face. And it's all your fault, missy!"

"How do you get that?"

"Wingate wants his revenge. If you hadn't of divorced the man, he wouldn't be taking out his spite on everyone connected to the farm!"

Doyle got the feeling Leigh was aching to launch herself at the trainer, fist first.

"Harley, enough!" Vanessa said coldly. Though she looked as if all the blood had drained from her, she shook Leigh's hands from her shoulders and stood. "I'll speak to you in private now. Your office." Without waiting for his response, she turned to Doyle. "Ashleigh has this urge to protect me, but I expect more from you. Anything you know, I want to know. And anything you need, don't hesitate to ask."

His respect for Vanessa's inner strength multiplying, Doyle said, "That goes two ways."

She nodded and started off, calling, "Harley," without looking his way.

And damned if the trainer didn't follow her like a pup being brought to hell.

"That Harley can be a pain in the butt," Thane muttered, giving Leigh a penetrating sideways glance, "but he is one helluva trainer."

Leigh was still burning with anger at the accusation that helluva trainer had thrown her way! And in front of Doyle McCoy, of all people.

"There are other good trainers," she returned, refusing to look at Doyle. Leigh didn't want to see what she guessed would be that mocking expression that she seemed to inspire. "Better ones than Harley. Ones who don't have a disposition worse than an ornery stallion."

Thane chuckled. "Sometimes he does remind me of old Wind Tunnel. Always ready to bite or kick or throw someone who's riding him. But Harley Barnett's always been loyal to this farm and your family, girl, especially in times of trouble. You remember that when you take over."

So the farm's reputation had dwindled along with ready cash. Not seeing how Harley had risen above anybody else just because *he* was sticking around, Leigh shook off the guilt trip Thane was aiming her way.

"Harley hates me," she reminded him. "When you retire, he'll probably up and leave on his own. Or haven't you heard the rumblings?"

"I heard. Don't necessarily believe 'em, though. First of all, he don't hate you. More'n likely, he's jealous. And if'n he left, he wouldn't get to see your mama every day, now would he?"

With that startling revelation, Thane ambled away, leaving Leigh gaping after him.

"I must be hearing things."

"Vanessa is an attractive woman," Doyle said, reminding her of his presence.

"Not you, too." Leigh flashed him an appalled look. "Mama wouldn't have anything to do with Harley Barnett, not personally. She had Daddy."

"Your father died years ago," Doyle reminded her. "Your mother didn't."

Leigh wanted to whip into Doyle, not for intimating her mother might have human needs, but that she might soothe those needs with Harley. Surely Mama didn't think of him as more than an employee. Then again, she remembered all the times she'd complained about the trainer's attitude toward her... and how her mother had always defended him. And when she'd suggested changing trainers, Mama wouldn't hear of "such nonsense."

"Oh, Lord, you don't think she'll marry him, do you?" The thought tortured her.

"Aren't you jumping the gun? Thane merely suggested Harley was sweet on Vanessa."

Doyle was obviously trying to make her feel better, but Leigh found it near impossible to back off. Her suspicions were aroused. Mama hadn't been home the night before. How many such nights had Leigh missed? And if Harley and Mama had a thing going—she refused to consider the word *affair*—when had it started? After she'd divorced Keith, putting the future of the farm in question? Did Harley care about her mother or what she could give him?

From the start, Leigh had absolved Harley of any guilt in the drugging incident because it didn't make sense that he'd blow his chance to have a colt win the Kentucky Derby. But what if he was counting on everyone buying into that? He'd figure he would be cleared because heroin was so obvious any trainer in his right mind wouldn't use the stuff to win. Maybe he had bigger stakes in mind than the Derby and had concocted some convoluted plan to get what he wanted.

What if Harley wanted Wind Racer Farm even worse than Keith?

What else might he be willing to do to get it?

DOYLE WAS NOT SYMPATHETIC to her point of view, a fact that put Leigh in a down mood as they arrived at Keeneland for another go-round. He wanted to pursue the fixed-race angle with those in the know.

When he headed for the clubhouse, she said, "I thought you wanted to talk to more people on the backside."

"I know people on *both* sides of the track."

He said it like a challenge. Not up to fighting, Leigh fell silent and lengthened her stride to keep up with him. Once in the clubhouse area, he slowed but didn't stop. His gaze swept the crowd as they moved.

"So, who are we looking for?"

"Lamar Graspin. He's a bookie."

"A bookie!" Leigh grabbed Doyle's arm. "He works here, at the track?"

"When he's in the mood. Lamar is an in-your-face kind of guy. And I saw him coming from the backside right before the Blue Grass. Didn't remember till this morning."

"How do you know him?"

Doyle stared at her steadily. "How do you think? Lamar started taking my money when I was a teenager, too young to place a legal bet."

Leigh had temporarily managed to forget Doyle had a problem with gambling. "I thought you said you hadn't played the ponies in almost a year."

"I haven't. Not until today."

"So now you're going to start betting again?" She couldn't say why it should, but the idea disturbed her.

"Only if we find Lamar."

"What are you thinking of?" Leigh demanded, then looked around quickly to make certain no one was tuned into their conversation. Not an eye was turned to them, yet she lowered her voice to be safe. "Dealing with a bookie is risky. Besides, you can't just start betting again.''

''I don't intend to get back into the habit,'' Doyle patiently told her. ''But if I want Lamar to talk, I'll have to offer him some incentive.''

''This is crazy.''

''So's Jimmy's being dead.''

But the explanation didn't soothe Leigh. She tried to tell herself that what Doyle did with his money was of no concern to her, and that she had nothing against people placing bets...as long as they didn't get carried away and lose more than they could afford.

But if Doyle noticed that his intentions upset her, he didn't let on. He moved to a nearby vacated table and picked up a discarded *Daily Racing Form*. Quickly scanning the past performances of the horses competing in the next couple of races, he tapped one of the entries and threw the paper back down on the table.

''Now all we have to do is find Lamar,'' he said.

''I don't think you should place that bet.'' Leigh grasped his arm and made him face her. She didn't know why it was so important to her that he listen to reason, but her stomach was knotted and her throat went dry. ''If you do this, you're asking for trouble.''

He shook her free. ''I can handle it!''

Startled by the brief explosion, Leigh sank into silence and followed Doyle as he started through the crowd again. His expression was as stiff as his back and she thought he might just keep walking.

Away from their investigation.

Away from her.

A minute later, however, he stopped and pointed to an area far removed from the betting windows but in full view of the field where horses were being loaded into the starting-gate chutes. "There he is."

Leigh followed his gesture to a table occupied by two men of far different years. The older one, perhaps in his fifties, had to be Lamar Graspin. Though dressed in an expensive sports jacket, he looked rumpled, and his graying hair escaped from under a crummy old felt hat that he probably wore for luck.

Doyle pressed his hand into the small of her back, and they moved closer as out on the track the gates opened and the pounding of hooves signaled the start of the race.

Leigh turned away from the field and focused on the second man at the table. Lamar's customer. Underage and nervous-looking, he slipped an envelope stuffed with something—money?—into a magazine which he passed to the bookie. Lamar slid the magazine into a leather attaché, made a notation in his Day Runner, then scribbled something on a slip of paper and slid it back across the table.

The younger man looked around as if checking to see if anyone was watching. But the crowd was focused on the race. When he spotted Doyle and Leigh approaching, he said something to Lamar in a tone that couldn't be heard above the enthusiastic shouts around them. Rising, he palmed the slip of paper and skulked off fast as the horses came down the stretch.

"Hey, Lamar, how's it going?" Doyle nearly shouted, stopping within spitting distance of the weasel-faced bookie.

Ignoring the now-screaming crowd, Leigh felt distaste as she watched Lamar Graspin chomp down on a cigar.

Lamar stood and watched the horses cross the finish line before saying, "Doyle, been some time." Eyes set too close together narrowed as he held out his hand to Leigh. "Lamar Graspin." She stared at the gold ring fashioned like a tiny racing saddle and the gold watch whose face was a horse enclosed by two diamond horseshoes. "And you are ... ?"

"Leigh."

She didn't offer her hand in return. Obviously getting the idea she didn't intend to, he let his drop.

"Park it." The bookie indicated the free chairs at his table as he himself sat.

Doyle didn't hesitate, and Leigh covered her reluctance. She didn't approve of what he was doing, but maybe she should trust him. Maybe he was only doing exactly what he'd indicated—bribing the bookie for information by placing a bet. For his sake, she hoped so.

"So what's your pleasure, Doyle?" Lamar puffed on his cigar.

"Sugarman in the eighth."

"A long shot, eh?"

Doyle's gaze met Leigh's when he said, "Sometimes a long shot pays off in a way you don't even expect. That makes it a risk worth taking."

For a moment, Leigh read more than business into his words. She felt as if Doyle were speaking directly to her on a very personal level. Her pulse sped up and she sensed something delicate hanging between them. Then Doyle turned to Lamar and the fine thread snapped.

"How much of a long shot?" he asked.

"Oh, I'd say...thirty to one."

Leigh tried to tune out and watch a fresh string of horses enter the track, escorted by riders on ponies. The men skirted around the issue, Doyle never directly saying he was placing a bet, Lamar never directly saying he was taking Doyle's money. But in the end, she knew it was a done deal though nothing changed hands. It seemed to her that Doyle's credit must be great. A thousand dollars' worth, anyway.

Leigh had to bite the inside of her lip to keep silent.

A thousand dollars thrown away and Doyle's addiction fed. What next?

"Odd how all of a sudden you're more interested in my operation than in the house system," Lamar drawled. "I'da sworn you outgrew me when you turned legal."

"I did," Doyle said, surprising Leigh, who'd assumed he'd been placing bets with the bookie all along.

Lamar seemed satisfied with the answer. He leaned back in his chair and turned the gold ring on his finger. "Then what is it you really want?"

"Information."

"Figures."

"About the Blue Grass Stakes."

"That figures, too." Lamar sighed and shook his head. "Poor Jimmy."

"You really feel badly?"

"He made money for me."

"Of course," Leigh murmured, at which the bookie merely raised a graying eyebrow.

"Then tell me what you know," Doyle urged.

"Be more specific."

"I got to thinking about why someone would give heroin to High Flyer. Not to ensure a win. There had to be another reason—to better the odds on Typhoon, for example." Doyle wasn't beating around the bush now. He glued his gaze on the bookie in challenge and demanded, "Tell me, Lamar, was the race fixed?"

Chapter Seven

If Lamar Graspin was surprised or felt put on the spot by the question, he didn't show it. Doyle looked hard but couldn't see a single crack in the bookie's composure.

"If there had been a fix, I woulda known." Lamar held out his hands in a falsely modest gesture. "My sources are impeccable, so that theory's nothing but gas."

The two men stared at each other in silence for a moment, Doyle finally saying, "I had to ask."

"Expensive question!" Lamar said, grinning.

But Doyle wasn't amused and he didn't care about the money. "Jimmy was worth it." And he didn't necessarily believe he'd bought the truth, either.

The crowd around them was growing restless again. Lines at the pari-mutuel windows were lengthening. Bettors came away, excitement over their wagers compensating for the fact that their wallets were a little lighter. Almost time for the next race. And for them to back off.

"Leigh," said Doyle, preparing to leave.

She practically flew to her feet and didn't even try to hide her relief as she edged away from the table.

"Good doing business with you again, Doyle. Don't be a stranger." The bookie turned a mocking smile on Leigh. "And proud to meet *you*."

Something about the way he said it made Doyle believe Lamar knew exactly who she was. He wrapped his fingers around her arm and cut through the crowd, but when she would have kept going directly to the exit, he encircled her shoulders and pulled her behind a support pillar.

She tried to shrug him off, demanding, "What do you think you're doing?"

He tightened his grip and realized he liked the feel of her against his side. "Playing a hunch."

That set her off. "A thousand dollars! I can't believe you bet a thousand dollars like...like it was something you did all the time!"

"I used to."

What he wouldn't admit was the thrill that had shot through him as he made the wager, even knowing that he was undoubtedly throwing his money away on an almost-ran like Sugarman. For a short moment, he'd forgotten he was doing it for Jimmy.

Leigh was trying to slither out of his grasp but was only succeeding in making him physically uncomfortable. Part of him wished they were somewhere private, somewhere he could indulge a few of the whims he'd been getting concerning her.

"*Will* you let go of me!"

He doubted if she'd appreciate having her mouth closed with a public kiss, though he was sorely tempted to give it a try. "Only if you promise to stay put and out of sight," he said instead.

"All right." Following the direction of his gaze back to Lamar's table, she immediately settled down, and he reluctantly released her. "What do you expect to see?"

"I'm not sure, but try to be patient."

That was like asking a dog not to eat a bone you'd put in front of his nose. Leigh shifted from foot to foot and did a lot of sighing, but he had to give her credit that she didn't bug him to death while he waited for Lamar to make a move. And waited. And waited some more. Doyle was beginning to think he'd been dead wrong, when a potential customer approached and the bookie waved him off.

"Yes!" he muttered.

"Yes, what?"

Leigh stepped out of the shadow of the pillar, and Doyle felt compelled to reel her back in. Against him, her back to his front. "Watch," he croaked hoarsely. She didn't struggle, content to snuggle back deep and let his body shelter hers.

Doyle tried not to get distracted as Lamar tested the crowd with his gaze. Then the bookie slipped his Day Runner, track program and *Daily Racing Form* into his attaché. Another look around. He rose and stretched, stuffed his cigar in his mouth. Smoothed his rumpled sports jacket. Flattened the brim of his old felt hat. Jerked his neck one way, then the other, like a furtive animal. Only then—when he seemed absolutely certain that no one was watching him—did he pick up the attaché case and slink off like the weasel he was.

Leigh started to move, as well. Doyle snaked an arm around her waist and tortured himself some more. "Not yet," he said, his lips so close to her ear he was tempted to taste it. "We don't want him to spot us."

She glanced at him, her waterfall of hair running over his arm, leaving him with gooseflesh. "We don't want him to get away, either. Right?"

He didn't want *her* to get away, but he had to concentrate on his mission. A few more seconds and Lamar was on the verge of being swallowed by the crowd.

"Now."

They moved as if with one mind, not getting too close, yet keeping the bookie within the periphery of their vision. He seemed intent. Focused. On what? Rather, on whom? They followed him for what seemed like forever. The crowd swelled, finally devouring the bookie whole. Doyle grew edgy the second he lost sight of the graying head.

"Damn! Where'd he go?" Doyle muttered, speeding up.

"This way."

Leigh grabbed his hand and jerked—her turn to muscle him in a slightly different direction. She steered him toward the private boxes. A few seconds later, Doyle zeroed in on the target. Victory flushed through him as, ahead, Lamar made the contact Doyle was hoping for.

"Well, what do you think of that?" Doyle asked.

Leigh snorted derisively. "I'm not exactly surprised. A long time ago, I realized my ex-husband was something to be picked from a horse's shoe."

For before their eyes, Keith Wingate shook hands with Lamar Graspin and invited the bookie into his private box. Doyle was barely close enough to see Wingate's pleasant visage change dramatically as Lamar did some fast talking.

If looks could kill. . . .

KEITH WINGATE ADOPTED that same grimace later that evening when he spotted Leigh entering the funeral-home foyer ahead of her mother and Doyle, convincing Leigh that Doyle had been correct—Lamar had shared the race-fix theory with her ex-husband. Whether or not it was true was still to be determined, but the odds were definitely in their favor.

Unable to help herself, Leigh brushed by the man she'd once cared for, sweetly murmuring, "That suck-egg expression you're wearin' spoils your carefully cultivated image, Keith, darlin'."

"Then I'll have to change it."

Amused that for once he sounded on the defensive, she added, "Actually, I think it suits you." She marched on, feeling his razor-sharp glare cut into her back.

"Ashleigh, this is not the appropriate time or place to indulge in angry words with Keith," her mother whispered as she caught up to Leigh.

"Don't worry, Mama, my baser instincts are assuaged for the evening."

"Your fine perception," Doyle corrected, murmuring the words in her ear as he flanked her other side.

He gave her shoulder a quick squeeze, then let his arm drop to his side, leaving her feeling empty somehow, even in the midst of a crowd.

The largest parlor had been reserved for Jimmy's wake, and rightly so, for people not only filled it, but spilled out the open doors both into the hall and onto the side terrace. Allowing the gravity of the evening to wash through her, Leigh took a deep breath and a better look around. Owners and breeders stood shoulder to shoulder with grooms, exercise riders and hotwalkers. All looked equally sober. And mournful. Everyone had loved—or, at least, respected—Jimmy Diaz. For this one night, there was no division of ranks between the clubhouse and the backside.

Thinking about the reality of that situation made Leigh twinge with discomfort, for hadn't Doyle drilled the facts into her again and again, even before she'd declared her love for him at age thirteen. She'd always denied the segregation existed, but in reality, it suited most involved. That she was an exception rather than the rule—no matter what Doyle believed!—saddened her almost as much as the flower-shrouded coffin across the parlor.

She was forcing her emotions in check by the time they arrived at the front of the room, where they gave their condolences to Jimmy's sister. Carmen had flown in to escort his remains back to Florida the next day for the actual funeral and burial.

Then there was no helping it, no getting away from facing the man who had been working for *her* when he'd had the accident that had taken him. Not an accident, she reminded herself. Deliberate intervention. Which equaled murder.

Leigh took a deep breath and stepped forward toward the coffin, which was covered with a blanket of roses declaring him a winner. Reminding her that he should have been riding the Kentucky Derby winner this year. Settling her gaze on the opening, she froze. Rather than a suit, Jimmy had been laid out in jockey's silks—the purple and yellow of Wind Racer Farms. Her first instinct was to protect her mother, but the older woman had already seen and remained calm and accepting.

"Mama, the silks—"

"I gave Carmen my permission. I thought buryin' Jimmy in them would be appropriate."

"That's the way he would have wanted to be remembered," Doyle agreed.

As did Leigh. But she couldn't force the lump down her throat to say so. Staring at Jimmy decked out in those silks, his jockey's cap tucked under one arm, she almost imagined he would pop up and say he was ready for his next race. Leigh tried to take heart. If there was a heaven, Jimmy would be riding for eternity....

A pressure on her arm made her look up at Doyle. He seemed to be having trouble swallowing, too. For a moment they were in tune in their shared sorrow. Then they moved on, allowed the next set of mourners their goodbyes.

Realizing her mother was crying silently, Leigh hugged her and heard her whisper, "My fault."

"Mama, don't you go blaming yourself." Which, as owner of Wind Racer Farm, she would. "You couldn't have known anything was wrong with High Flyer."

But *she* had. And had almost forgotten. The reminder strengthened Leigh's determination to ferret out the person who had drugged the colt.

Her mother was dabbing at her eyes with a lace-trimmed handkerchief when Harley elbowed through the crowd and solicitously said, "Vanessa, you all right?"

A brave smile quivered on Mama's lips. "I'll be fine, Harley, thank you. But I could use a cool drink."

Disliking the way her mother was looking at the man, Leigh volunteered. "I can get you something, Mama."

"Oh, Ashleigh, please stop fussin' over me."

"Shall we?" Harley held out his arm, which her mother took.

"You leave whenever you want," she told Leigh. "Harley will see me home."

And as they edged through the crowd together, Leigh told herself not to stew over it. Unsuccessfully. That her mother might be taken with Harley Barnett ate at her, particularly since the trainer wasn't off the hook yet.

"What about you?" Doyle asked, a warm palm at the small of her back reminding her of his very solid presence. "Would you like something?"

"The reason Jimmy died."

Again the connection. Funny how something as cold as death could bring antagonists together. And could make her feel so warm inside.

"Now?" he asked.

Leigh nodded. "The sooner we start, the sooner we can lay Jimmy's ghost to rest."

Although she wasn't certain the last was true. She would never forget the scene at the track when High Flyer jumped the rail . . . nor the sight of Jimmy's broken body being carted away on the stretcher.

"Where do you want to start?"

Leigh caught sight of Desiree as she stepped up to the coffin. The jockey was saying her goodbyes to Jimmy with tears streaming down her face. She was digging in a shoulder bag, most likely for a tissue.

"Maybe I should talk to Desiree. She's been doing an awful lot of crying over Jimmy. Maybe she was close enough to him to know something of value."

Doyle nodded. "I'll circulate. Don't leave without me."

The demand sounded personal. That she didn't feel like arguing the point surprised Leigh. What didn't surprise her was the way Doyle turned into one of the "good old boys" once set loose among backstretch mourners. He disappeared into a sea of grooms, exercise riders and hot-walkers.

Forcing Doyle from her mind, Leigh noted the moment Desiree stepped away from the coffin.

"Hey, Desiree."

"Hey." Desiree blew her nose and appeared embarrassed to be caught at a weak moment. Her eyes were red-rimmed and swollen from crying. Again. It seemed as if she'd hardly stopped since she'd won the Blue Grass. Leigh wondered if Desiree might have had a personal, if private, relationship with Jimmy Diaz.

"You want to get some air?"

"I'd appreciate that."

As they crossed the room through the thinning crowd, Leigh got a clear view of Lamar Graspin and Oakes McCoy huddled together in a corner. That they seemed deep in conversation bothered her. First Lamar had run to Keith, now he was keeping Oakes enthralled. Leigh didn't like it. She didn't want to draw conclusions that would implicate Doyle's daddy. She was glad to get outside.

Only a handful of people lingered on the terrace. The two women sat opposite on a vacant bench backed by fragrant flowering lilac bushes that rustled as if they were chattering to each other.

"Anything I can do?" Leigh asked.

"Bring Jimmy back?" They both fell silent for a moment. Then Desiree drew herself together and took a shaky breath. "It's all my fault, you know...Jimmy's death.... I'm responsible."

Leigh tensed. "You knew High Flyer was drugged?" She jumped on the possibility. "Was it Keith?"

Desiree stared down at the fists balled in her lap. "I pulled Typhoon too close to the inside. He doesn't like being crowded. I could tell he was getting ready to bite...that must have made High Flyer panic."

So that's why Desiree had been so upset—she blamed herself. "The accident wasn't your fault."

The jockey finally looked at Leigh directly. "I've heard what people in the industry say about me, that I'd ride over anyone who stood in my way for a win. Well, I won, didn't I? Looks like they know what they're talking about."

Desiree started crying again and Leigh gave the smaller woman a comforting hug. "You're a terrific jockey, but you're a woman. They wouldn't say that about you if you were a man. Stop blaming yourself."

Desiree blotted her tears with a tissue. "What a tragedy. Everything changed in the space of a heartbeat. Jimmy dead, Harley suspended from training—" she looked at Leigh with sympathy "—and you without a colt racing in the Kentucky Derby."

Leigh couldn't believe her friend was worried about *her*. "High Flyer is recovering. We'll give him an easy workout tomorrow morning to see how well. I'm not giving up on the Derby yet."

"But Harley's suspension—"

"—will be lifted if he's found innocent." Leigh hoped she sounded convincing when she said, "All we have to do is catch the real culprit."

Desiree hesitated before saying, "Thane mentioned you and Doyle were working together on it," as if she were wondering if it was in good taste to broach the subject.

"We've found out a few things that may help. Doyle and I figure the situation isn't as simple as it seems, but it's only a matter of time before we put all the pieces together."

Though the other mourners had gone inside, leaving them alone on the terrace, Desiree lowered her voice. "Thane said something about a note you found indicating Jimmy was going to throw the race."

"It was a fake."

Leigh wished that Thane hadn't been so expansive merely because Desiree was an old friend. What if the wrong person had overheard? Keith or Lamar? Even now, she got the feeling that someone was watching . . . listening.

The funeral-home setting and eerie wind were spooking her into imagining things.

"The note supposedly was from Oakes," Leigh continued finally, ignoring the shiver creeping up her spine. "That's what they were arguing about when you spotted them near the paddock before the race."

"So, did either of you show it to that Mr. Kenney who's been grilling everyone?"

"No. I promised Doyle I would keep hold of it for a while. Oakes got one, too, asking him to meet Jimmy. I hope he can find it to prove his story. We figure someone was trying to set them up."

"How terrible."

Though she hated putting her friend on the spot, Leigh knew it couldn't be helped. "Desiree, what I asked before . . . about Keith . . . have you heard or seen anything to make you think he might have been involved in High Flyer's drugging?"

"No, nothing direct."

"But something."

Desiree shrugged. "It's just that he's always angry with you."

"He never said anything specific to make you think he'd try for revenge?"

"Well . . ." The other woman looked uncomfortable. "Keith said he didn't care what it took, but that he was going to teach you a lesson and win the Kentucky Derby. That's not exactly a threat."

No, but it had a certain ominous ring. Leigh was wondering who else Keith might have made rash claims to—and if he might have gotten more specific—when a loud snap from somewhere behind them made her jump.

"The wind," Desiree said with an odd laugh against a kind of shushing sound. "Probably broke a tree branch or something."

Or someone was listening in. Glancing over her shoulder, however, Leigh couldn't see any movement through the thick lilac bushes. The place was poorly lit, too, puddles of faint golden light among spooky shadows cast by the trees. Anyone could be back there or around the corner of the building, and she would never know from where she sat.

In case her suspicions were justified, she changed the subject. "Say, I don't remember seeing Claude inside."

"Daddy wouldn't come."

Half her attention still focused on who might be lurking nearby, Leigh asked, "Not feeling well?"

"No. He can't face the tragedy," Desiree said in a flat voice that brought Leigh around. "It hits too close to home."

"That's understandable." Leigh knew Claude had been lucky to land in a wheelchair rather than a coffin. How ironic Claude had been crippled on another Fly Like the Wind descendant. Breeze had been one of the last colts the Kentucky Derby winner had sired in his final season at stud. "I'm sure Jimmy's accident stirred up all kinds of terrible memories."

Desiree turned inward, spoke more to herself than to Leigh. "I worry about Daddy so. He drinks too much. And when he gets morose, he gets real serious about it. Gets ahold of soda-pop moon."

Though she hadn't seen the stuff around in years, Leigh knew Desiree was referring to moonshine made illegally in the hills and sold in recycled soft-drink bottles.

"Did he ever think about getting back into the business, maybe going into training horses?"

"I've tried to push Daddy in that direction for years, but my encouragement doesn't do any good. Says I'm nagging him. Says his life is over and that's that."

Leigh felt for Desiree. She couldn't imagine one of her parents giving up on life like that. Even when he was dying of lung cancer, her father had forced himself from his bed to oversee the work at least a few hours a day. Feeling tears gather at the back of her eyelids, Leigh said, "Listen, after Keeneland's meet ends, why don't we get together to do something fun?"

Desiree smiled. "You mean maul a mall like we used to?"

"Shopping marathons always did make us feel better when we were under the weather. How about the Monday after?"

Surely by then this whole thing would be over. Everyone at the farm would be in the clear, and she'd need a reason to celebrate. Or so Leigh hoped.

"Sounds great." Desiree rose. "I've got to get going. I want to get home and check on Daddy."

"Okay." Leigh purposely remained seated. "See you a week from Monday, if not before then."

Desiree had barely set foot inside the parlor before Leigh flew off the bench to face a potential eavesdropper. She rounded the lilac bushes to investigate. No one on the lawn. Nor was anyone lurking around the corner of the building.

A sense of disappointment swelled inside Leigh, and she stepped back toward the terrace without looking where she was going. Her high-heeled shoe caught on something in the lawn, making her wobble and catch herself. What in the world...? A snake hole? Stooping, she focused until she saw it—a long, thin track.

Two sets of them.

Like a wheelchair coming and going.

If Desiree hadn't sworn her daddy was at home indulging his miseries with moonshine, Leigh might think that Claude Walker had been spying on them.

Chapter Eight

"Yeah, cain't believe Jimmy up and bought the farm," muttered Carl Janks, an old-timer who'd lived on the backside of tracks across the country and had been hot-walking horses for nearly half a century.

Doyle still couldn't believe it, either. He'd been making the rounds of mourners, hoping that one of his father's cronies could shed some light on the situation. So far, no luck, and half the room had already cleared. Even Pop had left.

"Swore he had a guardian angel looking after him," Micah Finley was saying. "Guess his angel got caught napping on the job this time."

"Hah. His luck ran out is all." Ned Searle had worked as Jimmy's valet for nearly a dozen years. "Always was afraid it would happen someday."

"I didn't know Jimmy was superstitious," Doyle fibbed, hoping to direct the conversation.

"You kidding? He didn't take no chances," a dour-faced Searle stated with the voice of authority. "Covered all his bases, from praying in church to getting his tarot read before a big race. He even had routes from wherever he was bunking to the track down pat—

wouldn't vary 'em. Figured he could use all the help he could get."

"Now that I think of it, you're right," Doyle said, carefully turning the subject to good-luck mementos. "His first meet, Jimmy found this coin in the paddock right before getting a leg up. He slipped the coin into his boot and won the race. Swore he'd always wear it."

"Still wearing it now beneath his silks." Searle's expression was grave as he glanced at the rose-blanketed coffin. "It'll be buried with him."

"That's something—the way jockeys don't ever quite believe in themselves, thinking they need extra help no matter how good they are," Doyle prompted, glancing at the terrace doors as Desiree stepped inside, her progress brought to a halt by Keith Wingate. "Pop told me Rey Boudreaux stuffs a gris-gris under his hat."

Janks chuckled, his ebony skin wrinkling into a hundred folds. "That old Cajun would. Got a better one, though. Harry York once taped a rabbit's foot to his ankle. Don't know how he got his boot on, but his ankle swelled so much they had to cut the leather to get it off!"

Jockeys had to bury their good-luck pieces. Nothing personal was allowed to show, not even a watch.

"Someone used to wear a horseshoe." Doyle furrowed his brow and feigned concentration. So far he and Leigh had kept their silence about the gold charm they'd found, and he wanted to keep it that way. "Who was that?"

"I know Jennie O'Malley pins a diamond-studded gold spur to her undies." Micah winked. "Showed it to me personal at Saratoga last year."

"And Victor Medina wears those holy pictures on a string," Searle added.

They were getting away from what he wanted to know, and Doyle was getting desperate. "No one knows anyone who wears a horseshoe?"

"Hmm." Carl Janks frowned. "I remember some jockey wearing a tiny gold one years ago. Cain't quite get a handle on who." He tapped his shiny bald pate. "Memory box ain't what it used to be. It'll come to me, though."

A nearby blur caught Doyle's attention. Spine stiff as a poker, Desiree hurried out of the room, making him wonder what Wingate had said to upset her. He didn't have long to think on it, for a moment later, Leigh whipped inside. He could tell she, too, was agitated about something, though she was doing her best to put on a good face.

Doyle listened to the men with half an ear as Leigh realized she had his attention. She locked her eyes on him, then directed them toward the exit. He got the drift—she wanted to know if he was ready to leave. He'd talked to dozens of people to no avail. No point in dragging the evening out any longer, so he nodded, waved her over and said his goodbyes.

"Boys, catch you at the track."

"Listen, Doyle, you did right nice by Jimmy this morning."

Doyle knew Janks was referring to the tribute he'd written. "Thanks."

"Be lookin' for your column tomorrow," Micah promised.

"Tomorrow's back to business."

"For some it is," Searle said, reminding Doyle the valet was temporarily out of a job.

"They'll be beating down your door when they hear you're available." With that promise, Doyle made his retreat.

Leigh was waiting off to the side, looking every bit the bereaved belle in a modest if flattering black dress with a cowl neckline and swirly long skirts. She'd slicked her thick dark hair back into a sophisticated twist that left her near-perfect features in stark relief.

Emphasizing the mole near her mouth.

Making a man forget what he was about.

"Ready to leave?" she reminded him.

They exited to the foyer, but before they could complete their escape, a familiar voice stopped him in his tracks. "Hey, Doyle."

"Lamar." Hanging on to Leigh so she wouldn't keep going, Doyle turned to meet Lamar Graspin head-on.

"Been trying to catch up to you all night. You're a popular fellow." The bookie was talking to Doyle but looking at Leigh. "Must've talked to near every man in the room."

"What's on your mind, Lamar?"

"You don't know?" Lamar reached into an inside pocket of his suit jacket, drawing Doyle's gaze directly to his tie tack—a gold horseshoe dotted with a single diamond. Part of a set. He was wearing matching cuff links. When he withdrew the hand, it was holding a long, beige envelope.

"Sugarman was in top form this afternoon."

For a moment, all Doyle could do was stare. He'd forgotten about the bet, had already withdrawn the money to square himself with Lamar. But he'd won. Thirty-thousand dollars' worth. He hadn't meant to win. Hadn't meant to stir up all those old feelings—the righteousness that came to him every time he'd earned extra money playing the ponies for tuition or a car payment or a down payment on a house.

He hadn't gambled in a year.

Hadn't meant to win.

But he took the envelope and felt Leigh stiffen next to him as he stuffed the winnings in his pocket. "Can't beat those long shots."

"Let's discuss long shots more thoroughly. I'll be at the track tomorrow."

"I'll keep that in mind."

Throughout the exchange, Leigh didn't say a word, but her disapproval telegraphed loudly enough. As Doyle escorted her out of the funeral home, her mouth was set in a frown. Tempted to either kiss the scowl away or demand an explanation—what made her think she had the right to approve or disapprove of his actions?—he did neither. He waited until they were in the car and on the road back to the farm.

And then he ignored the envelope that nudged at him, making him want to rip it open and check the contents, and concentrated on their evening's work. "So what did Desiree tell you?"

"Unfortunately, nothing specific." Leigh's voice was as stiff as her posture. "If Keith's responsible, I truly don't think she knows."

"Then what *is* bothering you?" Doyle asked, deliberately adding, "Other than Lamar."

He could almost hear her grind her teeth before saying, "I kept getting the feeling we weren't alone. That someone was spying on us."

"Did you actually see anyone?"

"After Desiree went inside, I investigated. I didn't find anything but tracks across the lawn to the sidewalk."

"Tracks," he echoed.

"That could have been made by a wheelchair."

Only one person came to mind. "Claude? He wasn't even there."

"At least you and I didn't see him. I went all the way around the building. He could have slipped inside through another door."

"Did you check the parking lot for his vehicle?"

Desiree had bought her father a van and had had it rigged special so Claude could be independent. It had not only hand controls, but a motorized platform that lifted him, wheelchair and all, to the driver's side.

"It didn't occur to me to look for the van," Leigh admitted. "Doyle, the thing I can't figure is why he'd want to spy on us."

"Maybe he was waiting for a chance to get Desiree alone."

"I thought of that, too. Makes sense, I guess, especially if he was juiced."

Leigh repeated what Desiree had told her about Claude's problem with alcohol and how it got worse when he was reminded of his own accident. And Doyle shared what he had learned—that maybe Carl Janks would remember who he'd seen wearing a gold horse-shoe charm.

"We seem to be getting nowhere fast," Leigh said in disgust.

"It's only been two days."

"Two *long* days."

Leigh wiggled her bottom around in her seat a bit, as if she was having trouble getting comfortable. The swish of material offered an invitation that Doyle forced himself to ignore. He clenched the steering wheel with both hands.

"You say that as if they haven't had their compensation. You and I are friends again." When she didn't jump to confirm, Doyle added, "Right?"

"Friendly acquaintances," she said somewhat grudgingly.

Doyle grinned and glanced her way. "Is that why you give me those looks?"

She gave him one right then. "You have an active imagination."

"I'm a writer," he agreed, "which makes me more fanciful than most. But I deal in facts, not fiction."

"Really." She hesitated only a second. "You deny facts when it suits you."

"What?" Doyle didn't have a clue...unless she was talking about him believing his father.

"Making that bet."

Annoyed, he snapped, "I told you why I did it."

"You could have offered to pay Lamar for information."

"He would have been insulted."

"More fiction. *Delusion*," she amended. "Lamar would have taken your money, only you wouldn't have gotten the rush of betting, right?"

So he'd gotten a rush—that didn't mean he was going back for more.

"You're beginning to sound like my ex."

"Maybe she had a point."

"Believe what you like," he growled. "I know what I'm talking about when say I can handle it."

"That's why you took the money."

"I didn't know I was going to win, for God's sake." And he hadn't figured out what to do with the windfall.

"So that makes it okay?"

"Get off my back! What right do you have lecturing me when you own racehorses that people like me bet on?"

"I participate in a sport." Now *she* sounded annoyed.

"You owners all think you're above the rest of us poor shlocks, but where do you get the money to stay in the *sport?* From people who gamble."

Obviously disliking the contradiction, she said, "There's a difference between sport and obsession." She'd gone from ticked off to icy. "But you don't seem to get it."

He got it, all right. But he *was* in control. She didn't get *that*.

"We all have our blind spots, Ash, don't we?"

By the time Doyle pulled into the farm drive, they were no longer speaking. Leigh dug out her shoulder bag from where she'd stashed it under the seat before going into the funeral home. All without a word, she threw open the door and herself out of the car and gave him one of those looks again. He stared at her as she hesitated, as if waiting for him to speak, to fix things, but he was too damn angry to make the first move.

So, it seemed, was she.

Maintaining her frosty silence, Leigh slammed the door and stomped off toward the barns rather than the house. And Doyle floored the accelerator and tore off the property. He found himself on the highway before realizing they'd made no plans for the next day.

The thought left him feeling more hollow than he was comfortable with.

THE DAMNED NOTE was nowhere in Leigh's rooms. If she had it, she must be carrying it around with her. Only one way to get it, then.

Just getting rid of the note wasn't going to fix things, though. Doyle and Leigh were too far in. They'd been asking too many questions. Undoubtedly getting too many answers, though they might not recognize that yet.

Why in the hell did they have to get involved and complicate the situation? Nothing was going as it should. Things had gone wrong from the get-go.

But that could be fixed.

Leigh could be fixed.

Tonight.

LEIGH WAS RUNNING OFF her fury with Doyle McCoy, ignoring the impending rain as she headed for High Flyer's barn. She wanted to see for herself if the colt was ready for a workout the next morning. She wanted to forget the argument.

She was sick of Doyle's continuing insinuation that as an owner she believed she was better than he.

But even more, she was angry at his wasting himself.

Why should she even care? Let him become a broken-down horseplayer if that's what he wanted! BDHs haunted the track day after day, season after season, always looking for that big score that would prove they'd been making wise "investments" rather than throwing away their money.

Thirty thousand dollars. That was big enough to inflate anyone's ego. Big enough to make someone who thought he was in control lose it.

And it would be her fault.

Cresting the rise in the road, she directly faced the wind, which forced her to slow down and take hold of her billowing skirts. The heavy air pressed against her like the guilt that was multiplying.

If only she'd refused to let High Flyer run when she'd sensed something was wrong, the colt wouldn't be hurt, Jimmy wouldn't be dead, Mama wouldn't be on the verge of collapse, Harley wouldn't be suspended and Doyle wouldn't be making wagers that would suck him back into a way of life that had no reward at the end of the road.

She *did* care, damn it! No matter that she wasn't supposed to. No matter that she wasn't thirteen anymore.

Lightning split the sky in the distance and thunder rumbled through the night, drawing anxious whinnies from the barns. Leigh's anxiety built, as well. She attributed her sudden case of jitters to the stress of the evening.

Ironic, the number of people blaming themselves, she thought, eyeing the sky filled with ominous dark clouds. She. Desiree. Mama.

Mama.

Leigh still hadn't had that talk with her mother, the one where she would coax an explanation as to why Mama wanted out of the business.

The atmosphere crackled and popped, and a tendril of apprehension urged her into High Flyer's barn. If she hurried, she could beat the storm back to the house. Nervous whinnies greeted her before she even flipped on the barn light. In an attempt to soothe, she talked to and touched each of the four colts stabled there, approaching High Flyer last.

"Hey, Bad Boy, how are you doing tonight?"

The colt was snorting and talking to her and prancing before she even hung her shoulder bag on a hook and opened his stall door.

"I know, you don't like storms, do you?"

A noise outside that didn't sound storm-related made her stop and listen intently. The wind blowing a loose door or shutter on one of the other buildings, maybe. She let out her breath.

"It's scary out there, but you're inside, all nice and safe and warm."

Anyone listening would think she was nuts, trying to talk sense to an animal. The words made Leigh feel better. What mattered to the colt was her presence, her tone of voice, her hands running gently over the hide that flinched and trembled and finally settled.

The cuts were healing. The injured foreleg looked and felt normal. No swelling. No sensitive spots. Leigh led High Flyer out into the aisle between stalls, turned him, then walked him back into his box. No limp, either, thank God. A restricted workout would reveal any weakness without doing the colt further injury.

She should have trusted Harley.

The thought raised some contradictions. Trust him with High Flyer's welfare now, but not about the drugging? Trust him with her colt, but not with her mother?

Leigh shook her head at the big beast who was nothing more than a baby, no matter how many hands he measured, no matter how fast he ran. ''I don't know what to believe in.'' High Flyer nudged her, snorted against her chest, leaving a smear across her dress—his expression of affection. ''Except you, Bad Boy. Sweet dreams,'' she whispered, quickly kissing the colt on the nose.

She was securing his stall door when another noise from outside startled her, this one too close to have come from another barn. Her heart pounded up into her throat. Someone had to be out there. She told herself to calm down, that being spied on at the funeral parlor had her jumpy for nothing, that someone was merely checking on the horses. Harley or Thane or Micah.

Switching off the light, she swung open the heavy barn door and slipped outside as splatters of rain finally tore free from the storm clouds.

"Harley?" Leigh secured the barn as a fat drop hit her between the eyes and careened down her nose. "That you?"

Only there was no answer.

And damned little light to see by.

"Micah? Thane? Anyone?"

She whirled around, glaring at the barns peppering the area. The buildings loomed over her, their outside lights too faint to do more than cast limpid pools around their entrances. Anyone could be lurking between or behind.

Who?

She backed down the road, her sharp gaze searching the area for some tiny movement. For something out of place. Aside from the steady drizzle of rain, the lightning in the distance, the rumbling thunder following, the area was motionless and still. Imagination could be a wicked adversary, and as far as Leigh was concerned, she'd had enough for one night.

Blood coursing, pulse jagging, she ran for the house. A set of footsteps slap-slapped behind her, but she firmly told herself they were her own echoing off the buildings. A half laugh, half sob bubbled past her lips. So why didn't the anxious, exhausted sound come back to haunt her, as well?

Why did she suddenly feel so unsafe on the land that had never been anything but nurturing?

Already soaked, the ground tricked her with its slickness. She'd gotten only halfway to the rise when her foot slid. She went flying, catching herself only by the grace of God and a four-board fence. Rain rolling

down her face, she gripped the wood and glanced behind her.

Nothing breathing down her neck, no footsteps...
but who knew what dangers that dark and rain con-
spired to hide?

Then, from the other side of the fence, a rhythmic
blowing claimed her attention. Blowing countered by
an equally melodic clop-clopping. These were unmis-
takable sounds—a horse traversing the pasture. But a
horse shouldn't be out in this kind of downpour.
Though the stallions might be left outside in decent
weather, at the first sign of a storm of any conse-
quence, they were supposed to be stabled.

Thoughts of her own safety fled as she strained to see
the big body weaving by her so close she could feel his
heat. More than fifteen hundred pounds of live steam
scorched her and retreated.

Leigh tried to identify him, but it was too dark...and
she was too disoriented to be positive which pasture the
horse traversed.

Another check around made her as certain as she
could be that she was alone.

Leigh climbed the two lower fence boards and whistled for the stallion to return. She meant to calm him
so that she could get him to shelter. A gust of wind
nearly blew her off her feet. Balancing against it, she
leaned farther over the fence and into the pasture and
whistled again.

The stallion was moving through the small five-acre
field erratically now, whinnying his agitation.

She didn't blame him for being angry. Wretched
weather was something he was normally protected

against. She herself was soaked to the skin, chilled to the bone and weighted down by the sopping skirts of her dress.

"Hey, you old jughead," she called sweetly, her tone rather than the words meant to calm him. "Come on over here and I'll get you inside where it's warm and dry."

Lightning tore at the dark, and the stallion reared, letting loose an ear-piercing scream that nearly drowned out the responding thunder...

...and the suck of mud behind her.

Leigh tensed. Some night phantom had been lurking. Waiting. She whipped around.

Too late. A wall of pain stopped her.

And the world went even darker.

Chapter Nine

The earth pulled at her, held her glued facedown so she could scarcely breathe.

Close to suffocating, Leigh was barely able to turn her head. A mistake. The world lit and spun from within like a merry-go-round. When the ride slowed, she breathed in a ragged lungful of liquid air along with a smattering of mud and tried to remember what happened. She was dizzy and cold and wet. A steady rain drummed down on her back, but it did nothing to put out the fire searing the side of her head.

Where was she? Trying desperately to orient herself, she ran a palm across the ground.

Some mud. More grass.

Suddenly the earth rumbled and an animal scream slashed through the night . . . the same horrific sound she'd heard just before her world had cut out on her. That familiar shriek of dissatisfaction reflected a life-long spirit of meanness that had never been tamed.

"Wind Tunnel," she groaned.

Her head pounded, her world spun, but still she pushed herself into a sitting position. The hooves were coming straight for her. She couldn't see him, but she could hear. The stallion was terrified, and who knew what he might do? Of all the horses to have to deal with under any circumstances, Wind Tunnel would have been her last choice. And these were the worst circumstances possible.

Knowing it was her only chance to save herself, she yelled, "Ey-yah!" then squinched her eyes and clenched her teeth against the pain reverberating off the inside of her skull.

But it worked. Startled by the unexpected noise, the stallion sidestepped and dodged around rather than running right over her. She sensed his panic and fought from making it her own as he circled the enclosure, every so often brushing against the fence, making some of the looser boards clatter.

Leigh attempted to rise to her feet but merely made it to her knees before stopping to regain her equilibrium. Someone had hit her in the head—now she remembered—and then she must have fallen into the pasture....

But when she swayed to her feet and held out her hands, she couldn't find the fence. She tested different directions, even taking a few shaky steps this way and that, but she didn't seem to be near it at all.

How could she have fallen so far?

The thunder of hooves was coming straight at her again. Wind Tunnel was acting crazed—even for him. Leigh couldn't help but be afraid. She gauged his bearings and tried to move out of his way, but he dodged in the same direction, clipping her hard in the shoulder. She went flying...and finally found the damn fence!

Stunned, she wrapped her arm around a post so she wouldn't slide back to the ground. She didn't know if she could make it to her feet a second time. If only she could focus, could see *something*.

A beam of light.

At first she thought she'd conjured it. More carnival rides. The light bobbed and swayed. But there was only one. A flashlight. A new danger. Whoever had attacked her was returning!

She had to get out of there. Clawing her way along the fence, she searched for the gate. No way would she try climbing the fence in her condition. She'd kill herself for sure.

The light shone closer.

Leigh had no idea where she would hide. At least she could run. At least she could try. The gate. Hands desperately searching for the latch, she was distracted from the light for a moment by Wind Tunnel coming around for a third pass. He was moving slower and sounding badly winded. She turned back to the gate just in time to have the flashlight blind her. And the stallion.

The scene played out in slow motion. With a half-hearted squeal, the horse reared, front hooves slashing through the beam of the flashlight as they came straight for her.

Mesmerized, she froze.

And the gate jerked open, throwing her off balance yet again. Steel fingers grabbed her upper arm and whipped her from the pasture. She fought blindly, swinging her free arm, catching the man with a fist.

"Whoa!" Strong arms whipped around her. "It's me." The bobbling beam of the flashlight illuminated his face.

"Doyle?" She'd never been so happy to see anyone in her life. She took comfort in the strength and warmth of his arms, the concern she'd heard in his voice. For a moment. Long enough to regain her composure. Then she blew. "What the hell were you trying to do, scaring me like that?" She pushed at his chest until he let her go.

"I thought I was saving you."

"You could have identified yourself."

"You could have asked me to," he returned. "Who did you think it was?"

"I don't know. The person responsible for my being trapped in there with the farm demon in the first place."

"Huh?"

"Wind Tunnel," she explained. "We have to get him out of there and into his barn."

"What do you mean by the person responsible—"

"After we get the horse."

"Now."

She grabbed the flashlight out of his hand. "He's acting so crazy, I'm afraid he'll break a leg or something if we don't get him calmed down and out of there."

Doyle conceded the argument and set to help her. Corralling the stallion took coaxing and time, but, obviously exhausted and wanting to be pampered as usual, Wind Tunnel finally allowed himself to be captured. Leigh confiscated Doyle's belt and attached it to the horse's harness. She didn't let down her guard for a single moment, and rightly so, for in gratitude, the stallion showed his teeth and tried to take a chunk of her arm.

Snapping the makeshift lead, she muttered, "Ingrate!"

Leigh led Wind Tunnel back to his barn where Doyle helped her secure the horse in the aisle between stalls. Finding a couple of towels, she threw one to Doyle.

"Watch his feet." She began wiping down the stallion. "He still likes to kick, too."

Working on the other side, Doyle brought the conversation back where she'd cut it off. "Is he the one who landed you in the pasture?"

"Not unless he snuck up on me and whacked me in the head first."

Doyle circled the aisle and pulled her away from the horse. He grabbed her chin, aimed her face to the light and looked into her eyes. "Pupils are normal. Doesn't look like a concussion. How does it feel?"

"Like a carnival ride," she breathed, only this time she wasn't seeing lights. His touching her was making her insides tumble. And it shouldn't, not after their argument. "Why did you come back?"

"Turn your head." Though he explored her scalp gently, she winced when he found the spot where she'd been hit. "I didn't want to leave things the way they were between us." He pulled his hand from her head. His fingers were bloody. "You need a doctor."

Her head hurt like hell. Her skin was clammy. But it was her chest tightening with emotion that bothered her the most.

"Head wounds bleed a lot. It doesn't mean anything." Or so she'd heard somewhere. "Besides, a doctor's not what I need right now."

"Then what?"

How could a man be so dense? Doyle's expression was questioning until he looked deep into her eyes. Then he seemed to understand. He slipped his arms around her and offered the comfort and warmth of his body. Leigh shuddered and moved closer. Wind Tunnel's hooves clacked against the barn floor and he snorted and whinnied impatiently, setting several other horses to answer. She ignored them all for the moment. She needed to be held. Reassured. Kissed.

"What happened tonight?" she murmured against Doyle's chest.

"We hit a crossroads of some kind. We got too close. Or someone thinks *you* did."

She shuddered. "Someone purposely tried to hurt me."

"If anything had happened to you . . ."

She drew away so she could see his face. "What?"

"I would have blamed myself."

Not exactly the romantic sentiment she craved. "Why?"

"Because I dragged you into this."

Guilt. She was familiar with that particular curse.

"No one can make me do something if I don't want to," Leigh said. "Is that it? Placing blame? Don't I mean anything to you *personally?*"

Rather than answer with words, he captured her face with both hands and kissed her. Really kissed her. Very *personally* kissed her.

Leigh reveled in the feel of his lips, his tongue, his teeth. She dropped the towel and wrapped her arms tight around his back. Something breaking free inside, she responded in kind. She'd waited more than half a lifetime for Doyle McCoy to kiss her! Her head went light and her knees felt weak and a hot aching started deep inside. More than her mouth was involved here, she thought with a moment's satisfaction.

She hadn't been kissed so thoroughly since...since Keith.

Leigh struggled free, muttering, "Keith!"

And Doyle tensed. "You're a little confused. The name's Doyle, remember?"

Tempted to punch him for that one, she restrained herself. "Certainly, I remember. Do you think I don't know who I'm kissing? I meant Keith might be the one who attacked me. I figured he never really cared, but I never suspected he might hate me enough to...to..."

Suddenly her teeth were chattering, and she went cold inside. Even Doyle cloaking her with his body couldn't warm her. Still, she had no urge to move until the barn door slammed open and a caustic voice said, "Well, isn't this a cozy scene."

That made her pull away from Doyle and face Harley Barnett, who stood in the opening, water dripping from his dark, hooded windbreaker. A flash of embarrassment at being caught in a weak moment heated her up enough that her cheeks flamed.

"What are you doing here?"

"I was on my way to the colts' barn," Harley stated. "Thought I'd check on High Flyer for the night before bunking in. Saw the lights and wondered what was going on in here." He looked from her to Doyle. "Seems my concern was for nothing."

"We were taking care of old Wind Tunnel here," Doyle told him.

Leigh quickly picked up her towel and began drying the stallion with so much vigor that he edged away from her. "He was left outside in the storm."

Seeming to notice the still-wet horse for the first time, Harley frowned. "No. He wasn't. I saw Xavier bring him in earlier."

"Maybe Xavier was bringing in Fly Like the Wind."

Hearing his name, the stallion who was Wind Tunnel's mirror image whinnied.

"I know what I saw!" Harley looked to have something more on his mind, but he abruptly turned and stalked out of the barn, muttering to himself.

And Leigh concentrated on Wind Tunnel so she wouldn't have to think.

"Someone brought this old guy outside." Doyle went back to helping her. "For what?"

"To distract me?" she guessed. Any hopes she might have had of this being a random attack, an attempt at simple theft, were shattered. "The person knew I would realize Wind Tunnel was out and that I wouldn't leave him there in the storm. I was set up." Reality was sinking in faster than she liked. "Someone tried to *kill* me, that's what."

Could that someone really be her ex-husband? Did Keith hate her so much for spoiling his plans for his professional future that he would want to see her dead?

"Leaving you in a pasture with a half-crazed horse is pretty nasty, but not a surefire way to commit murder." Doyle stared at her over Wind Tunnel's back. "Maybe he was only trying to stop you from investigating. And maybe he wanted something he thought you had."

"The note," Leigh said reluctantly.

As of that morning, several people knew about it. But not Keith. Or had someone told him? Someone from Wind Racer Farm? More likely, the informer might have been Oakes.

"The note was in my purse." She couldn't remember carrying anything as she fled for the house. "I must have left it in High Flyer's barn."

They stared at each other and Leigh knew Doyle was thinking the same thing as she—that Harley was on the way to that very barn right now.

"We'll go back for your bag after we make sure the demon here is properly cooled down and dry," Doyle said.

And Leigh wondered if they would be setting off on a fool's errand. . . .

"IT'S STILL HERE!" Leigh cried with relief.

Doyle stood in the doorway while she ran to the peg from which her shoulder bag hung. The sleepy colts nickered and turned around in their stalls so they could eye the humans. For once, Leigh didn't seem to notice what they were doing. She was digging through the bag, shaking her head, giving Doyle a sour feeling.

"What?" he asked.

"It's not in here."

"You're sure?"

She dumped the contents on a stool. Wallet, keys, makeup, tissues. No crumpled, grimy piece of stationery.

"How stupid can one person be?" she muttered to herself, scooping the articles back into the bag. "Why was I carrying it around with me? I should have found a safe place to hide the damn thing."

Knowing he likewise carried the gold horseshoe charm in his wallet, Doyle said, "Don't beat yourself up. We're not pros at this. We don't think like criminals. Guess we should have turned the evidence over to Kenney while we had the chance."

"Who took it? Harley? Was he the one who...?"

Doyle couldn't answer that any more than she could. He noticed Leigh was shaking and trying to cover herself. He didn't like that any more than he did her too-pale and drawn appearance.

"About that doctor—"

"No! I just need dry clothes and a warm bed. I'm beginning to feel like a drowned rat."

Stubborn, stubborn woman! Rather than argue with her, Doyle decided he would go back to the house with her and stay until he was convinced she was all right. And if she wasn't, he would *summon* a doctor, if necessary.

They quickly secured the barn and traded it for Doyle's car. When he'd turned back to the farm, the idea of chasing after Leigh in the rain hadn't held much appeal, so he'd driven across the property, keeping his window cracked and his eyes open. When he'd heard Wind Tunnel making a commotion and had realized something was wrong out in that pasture, he'd abandoned the vehicle nearby to investigate. Considering the way Leigh was starting to shake, he was glad they'd gone back for it before checking on High Flyer.

"At least the rain stopped," she said, trying to control a shudder.

Taking off his jacket, he held it out for her. "Here. No arguments."

Her smile was wan. "Thanks."

Doyle helped Leigh slip into the jacket, then wrapped an arm around her shoulders and pulled her close to his side, happy that he was able to provide the warmth she needed. As he drove toward the house, he analyzed his own tender feelings for this woman who'd gotten under his skin—and not always in a positive way—for as long as he could remember. Most of the time, Leigh seemed to need no one and nothing but this farm. But experiencing her like this, when her guard was down, when she was neither trying to be irritatingly independent nor to out-magnolia anyone, he couldn't resist her.

"Warm enough?"

"Feeling better." She snuggled deeper into his side.

It was becoming increasingly difficult to remember why he thought they couldn't be together. Doyle was relieved when they arrived at the house and broke the close contact, allowing him to think clearly once more.

"I'm going to take a quick shower," Leigh said, returning Doyle's jacket to him in the foyer. "Help yourself to the liquor cabinet."

Thinking he should be leaving, Doyle nevertheless found himself wandering toward the living room door. "I'll have a brandy if you will."

Halfway up the stairs, she yelled, "Deal," over her shoulder.

He watched her ascend and then round the corner before he headed for the liquor cabinet. He needed that drink, for he feared he was in real trouble.

He'd convinced himself he was falling in lust, but this latest incident convinced him his feelings for Leigh were more complicated—not that he hadn't worked up a physical thirst for her when he'd kissed her earlier. That he was veering out of control was scary, for there was nothing to be done about it. They really were from two different worlds, ones that existed shoulder to shoulder, perhaps, but each with its own rules, separated by a line that was rarely crossed.

He'd finished one brandy and was starting on his second when Leigh came downstairs wearing a thick blue terry robe, a matching towel wrapped around her head.

"That feels better."

"You *look* better." He handed her a drink, which she immediately tested. Not wanting her to get the drift of what he'd been thinking, he purposely said, "You were beginning to remind me of a drowned rat."

He wasn't certain if his words or the brandy put the color into her cheeks. She sank down onto the couch and gave him one of those looks of hers.

"Why, Doyle McCoy, are you makin' light of a woman who survived a gully washer and a stallion who's got more kick than liquid dynamite?'' she demanded, unable to hide a grin.

For a moment, Doyle grinned, too—Leigh seemed back to her normal self—but then her words sank in. Wind Tunnel was nastier than raw whiskey, and Leigh was lucky he hadn't injured her.

"I think tomorrow we should tell the authorities everything," he said.

A difficult decision, since his father was somehow involved in the mess. But one person was dead. He didn't want to take any chances with Leigh's life. She might not be so lucky a second time.

She swirled the remaining brandy in her glass. "I think we should sleep on it."

"Don't be foolish."

"If we go to Kenney or whomever the state brings in, we're just going to look foolish," she insisted. "We have nothing to back up our suspicions. We don't even have the note anymore."

"I don't want you to get hurt."

"I could get hurt no matter what we decide. I have this awful premonition, Doyle." Her eyes were wide, her expression serious. "That whoever's responsible isn't going to stop until the farm is destroyed... whatever that takes."

Doyle sat next to her, playing with the remainder of his drink. "Listen, Ash, I know this must be feeling real personal right now." It took all his willpower not to pull her into his arms and tell her how sorry he was he got her involved so deep.

She shook her head. "I don't think it's just about me. I'll be more careful, I promise. No more wandering around alone at night. If this *is* about the farm, you know we have a better chance of finding out the truth than an outsider."

That's the justification he'd used in the first place. But how was he to know he'd be putting Leigh in danger? "We could share the load with people who know how to run a professional investigation."

"And could politely be thanked while our suspicions are ignored." Leigh swallowed the last of her brandy and set down the glass. "We could even be told to butt out."

Doyle didn't know if she was really making as much sense as he thought or if he *wanted* to be swayed. "I'll sleep on it," he promised. He set his glass next to hers and got to his feet. "I'd better get going. I've got a column to finish." Though the idea was no more appealing than it had been earlier.

"I'll see you out."

But when they got to the foyer, rather than opening the door, she leaned against it. Her robe slipped open a bit, giving him a shadowy invitation he fought to ignore.

"Thank you for coming to my rescue," Leigh said, her tone sincere. "I'm sorry about getting on your case. About the bet, I mean. What you do is none of my business. I . . . I was concerned about you, is all."

That did it! Weakened him like nothing else could have. She couldn't have thought of a better way to make him want to stay. Well, maybe if she loosened the robe a little more. He thought to hush her mouth with his, swing her up into his arms and carry her upstairs as Rhett did to Scarlett. He'd even bet she'd like that.

"You're staring," she whispered.

"Am I?"

"If there's something on your mind, just up and say so... or do it."

She was challenging him! Doyle couldn't help himself. He moved in, flattened both hands on the door, one on either side of her face. Though he wasn't touching her, he could feel her heat. Some shower. Or maybe it was the brandy.

"You oughta be careful, Ash, giving open invitations like that." He was so close he could hear her breath coming in uneven spurts. Not unlike his own. And her eyes were wide and bright and inviting. "You don't know what you might be getting yourself into."

Her lips trembled into the tiniest of smiles. "Why, Doyle McCoy, after all these years, you haven't gone and taken a shine to me, have you?"

Leaning even closer, he feathered her mouth lightly. "That would be ironic, wouldn't it."

"Downright preposterous."

He ran his tongue along her upper lip. "We've never gotten along."

"Hardly ever."

Nipped her lower lip. "We should be content with mere friendship, right?"

"Undoubtedly correct."

Given all that logic, he shouldn't have kissed her again. Sometimes logic was a pain in the butt best left to handicapping, he thought, kissing her. She pressed against him, and he imagined that robe opened a bit wider, that he felt the swell of her bared breasts through his damp shirt.

"You'll get chilled again," he murmured without actually breaking contact.

He thought she said, "Not likely," but he couldn't be certain because then she was kissing him, making it impossible for him to get a word in edgewise even if he wanted to.

Which he didn't.

Gone with the Wind fantasies playing through his mind, Doyle explored the mouth that was still sassy even when it wasn't saying a thing. It plucked from him not only a quick, hot desire that he wished he could take forever to cool, but a longing that went so much deeper. That hankering for something more than passion drove an invisible wedge between them because he knew it was impossible to have.

Freeing his mouth, Doyle plucked at the edges of her robe and restored her modesty. "Wouldn't want your mama to be shocked," he teased, wondering where Vanessa was. Odd that she hadn't been around since they'd entered the house.

He sensed Leigh's emotional withdrawal as she moved to open the door for him. He couldn't help the disappointment that followed even though he knew it was for the best. They'd both been experimenting, just to see...

But as he prepared to brave the elements—it was raining again—she said, "Sleep on that, as well."

Disbelieving, Doyle brushed her lips one last time before he retreated into the night. A mistake. Getting too close would be a big one. He knew that, but knew it was a mistake he was bound to make, because he could no more stop himself from wanting her than he could stop wondering who was shaking up both their worlds.

And wondering where the culprit would strike next.

Chapter Ten

If Keith were the guilty one, maybe she could psych him out. That thinking brought Leigh back to Wingate Stud the next afternoon for the first time since her divorce. Wanting to handle this alone, she'd told Doyle she would meet him later.

The moment she drove onto the property, which was surrounded by a luxurious five-board white fence, she was reminded of the money that had blinded her to Keith's faults. To her shame, she couldn't say which she had found more appealing—the man himself or the fact that he had promised to help her realize her father's dream for Wind Racer Farm.

Rather than park near the monstrous house which Keith had designed with outclassing the competition in mind, she went on to the paved parking lot between the training facilities and the barns. Never quite knowing what to expect from her ex-husband, she left the car with some trepidation. To her surprise, she recognized Claude Walker's van and wondered if he was there with Desiree.

Outside one of the barns, Oakes McCoy was readying Typhoon for his daily bath. The groom noticed her, too. Waving, she jogged over to him. "Morning, Oakes."

"Ashleigh."

He seemed uncomfortable, no doubt due to her having been present when Doyle had questioned his father about the argument with Jimmy. He also knew she had been the one to find the now-missing note.

"I'm surprised to see Typhoon here," Leigh said.

Oakes jiggled the colt's bit to keep him occupied while an assistant groom turned on the hose. At the first splash of water on his hindquarters, Typhoon tried dancing away, but Oakes kept him in check.

"Mr. Wingate thought he might've strained a muscle. Brought him home for some water therapy."

In addition to a practice track, her ex-husband had built an indoor therapy facility, complete with equine swimming pool and treadmill. "He must be okay if he was working out."

"All clear. I'm bringing him back to Keeneland this afternoon," Oakes stated. "What about High Flyer?"

"He had a light workout this morning—his first since the accident. No problems, thank God."

And though she'd watched Harley closely during the workout, she'd had no indication that he wasn't as relieved as she. Probably more so. No matter that the trainer had access to her purse, she was leaning toward the theory of someone else having been in the colt's barn before him.

"Tomorrow, we'll push High Flyer a bit," she went on. "Assuming he checks out, he'll go back to Keeneland so he can start working on a full-size track again."

Leigh noticed the assistant groom stayed well away from Typhoon's back legs as he lathered the colt with a soapy liquid. The colt struck out, anyway, his hooves meeting thin air. So he was a kicker.

"You really think keeping up your hopes for the Derby is wise?"

The odd way he phrased the question alerted Leigh. "I don't think, Oakes. I know." And made her wonder if he were trying to tell her something.

Two exercise riders were just taking horses out to the practice track. She looked over to the bleacher area. A clocker was timing one of the horses already working out. She recognized the trainer who broke in the yearlings and worked with some of the less promising two-year-olds.

No Keith.

As she continued searching for her ex-husband, a dark shadow moved into her peripheral view. "You wouldn't know where your boss— Hey!" Leigh ripped her arm away from Typhoon, who'd nipped her hard.

"Sorry," Oakes said, snapping the lead to get the horse back under control. "Got to pay attention to this devil every minute. He get you good?"

Leigh was rubbing the spot. "No blood drawn, but I can add another bruise to my collection," she groused. "I never knew Typhoon had such a mean streak. Like Wind Tunnel." Her shoulder and hip were both bruised after her encounter with the old stallion. "You'd never know he and High Flyer were out of the same line."

"Mr. Wingate's in his office." Oakes's attention was now fully on the colt, who was being rinsed down.

And Leigh had the feeling of being summarily dismissed.

Wondering if she were imagining things, she strolled over to what had been the original home on the property before Keith had built the new one. He'd renovated the modest-sized house, had filled it with fine carpets and antiques and equestrian artwork. Nothing but the best. She was aiming for the side door to avoid Keith's secretary, hoping the element of surprise would work in her favor, when the door opened and Claude came wheeling out, Keith directly behind him.

Something made her pause under the shade of a leafy old tree rather than announce herself. As the two men approached, she realized they were in the midst of a heated discussion and didn't notice her.

"As far as I'm concerned, I've been more than generous," Keith was saying.

"A man like you could afford to be—"

"Mr. Wingate!" came a woman's voice, cutting off whatever Claude was going to say. His secretary came running down the path after him. "Oakes called to tell you that new filly arrived. She's in the main barn."

Leigh couldn't help wondering if the "new filly" were the four- or two-footed kind.

"Your time is up, Claude," Keith said, racing off, his focus on the main barn, so that while he practically ran past Leigh, he still didn't notice her.

"For now," the ex-jockey yelled after him. "We're not through yet."

Through with what? Leigh wondered. The words had an almost ominous ring. As far as she knew, Claude hadn't been working for Keith. Not if Desiree were correct about her daddy. Then again, Desiree was so busy with her career, and half the time she was based at some racecourse halfway across the country....

Claude rolled forward, and Leigh stepped out of the shadow of the tree as if she'd never meant to do anything else. "Hey, Claude." She would swear he started guiltily. "Where's Desiree hiding?" Walking alongside him, she got the feeling she made him uncomfortable.

"Don't rightly know." He checked his watch. "My guess'd be Keeneland."

Not at Wingate Stud. So Claude had come alone specifically to see Keith. Something about money. But for what? Leigh couldn't very well come right out and ask. Maybe she could work up to the topic.

"How is Desiree?" she asked instead. "She was pretty upset last night. At Jimmy's wake," she deliberately added, wondering if he would admit to having showed.

His expression closed. "She's doin' just fine."

Leigh pressed him. "She seems to be under so much stress over what happened."

"Who isn't?"

"But *she's* taking it personally."

"What's that mean?" Claude demanded.

"That Desiree blames herself for Jimmy's death. Surely she's told you that."

He spun those wheels faster, making her stretch her stride to keep up. "My girl didn't kill Jimmy."

"I didn't say that." But he'd denied it as if he knew who did. Keith? Was that what he wanted money for?

To keep quiet? "Desiree figures she let Typhoon get too close to High Flyer and spooked him."

"There some point to this conversation?" Claude was growing openly hostile.

"I'm concerned about your daughter—"

"Don't be!" he said harshly. "Look to your own family. Look close, missy, and then point fingers."

Leigh stopped dead in her tracks and stared after him. He kept on wheeling toward the parking lot without looking back. He certainly was touchy considering she hadn't been accusing Desiree of anything. And what was that crack about pointing fingers at her own family? Surely he wasn't accusing Mama of anything.

What *had* he and Keith been talking about?

Frustrated, Leigh realized she stood directly opposite the main barn. The doors at both ends were wide open and she could see straight through the shadowy main aisle. Keith was talking to one of the assistant grooms, probably giving him instructions on how to handle the new filly. Steeling herself for what she figured would be an unpleasant confrontation, she entered the barn.

Her boots clacked against the asphalt, alerting her ex-husband. Seeming genuinely surprised to see her, he quickly finished his business and waved off the groom, who left in the opposite direction. Keith strode toward her, meeting her halfway.

"Why, Ashleigh, honey, aren't you looking radiant."

His words held the hollow ring of falseness that had pervaded their marriage.

"And you're looking equally fine." Better, if the truth be known—but then, he always had.

"Compliments?"

"Passing time."

He hid his irritation behind that mask she knew so well. "Whatever brought you here must be important. I know how much you dislike Wingate Stud."

"Not the place. Just the head stud."

His veneer slipped. "What do you want?"

"The truth. I know you are unfamiliar with the concept—"

"Cut to the chase."

Leigh stared at him, hoping she could make him sweat inside. "I want to know exactly how much you hate me, Keith. How much you want to see Wind Racer ruined." She could tell he was working up to a glib answer, and she didn't give him the chance to use it. "I want to know if you paid Jimmy Diaz to throw the Blue Grass."

"What!"

She smiled sweetly. "You heard me, Keith, honey."

"What the hell is this? What are you plotting? Some kind of revenge?"

"Revenge is *your* specialty." She thought he might deny it; he didn't. "You can't have Wind Racer. And you don't want me to have it, either."

"True enough."

"So you admit it."

"What?" Moving toward her smoothly, he couldn't hide his acrimony. "That I've paid more than I should have to buy colts and fillies you and Vanessa wanted? That I could afford to double the rates of one of your favorite jockeys so she's unavailable to you?" The veneer vanished. "That I've had a little fun with the media at your expense?"

"That you fixed the race."

He circled her and, without actually touching Leigh, pushed her toward an opening. An empty stall.

"Don't even think it," he growled, slowly advancing.

Although Leigh was now getting truly nervous, she straddled the stall entryway and held her ground. "Too late."

"Your mind is warped. Comes from too much inbreeding."

Though the words sounded as though they were meant to be amusing, his expression was anything but. Leigh had a second's pause to wonder what she was getting herself into. She'd come alone because she thought she might be able to taunt the truth out of Keith. She couldn't stop now.

"Or didn't Jimmy go for your deal?" she continued, despite the fear making her heart hammer. "Did he turn you down, Keith?" And her dry mouth made it difficult to speak. "Is that why you drugged High Flyer?"

Face diffusing with unflattering color, Keith loomed over Leigh and backed her into the stall. He was so close she could feel the vibrations of his anger. The wooden wall stopped her cold, and still he kept coming for her.

"Don't you have enough to do, keeping that mausoleum of a horse farm running?" He stopped a mere hair's breadth away.

Swallowing hard, she tried not to show her fear. "I'm the one asking the questions here."

His smile was feral. "Indeed, you are. I never knew you were capable of this much backbone, or you might have interested me more while we were married."

A fist unclenched and his hand stroked her cheek. Then her neck. And wandered lower.

Eyes wide, she struck his hand away and gave him a shove that left her with some breathing room. "Don't touch me."

"And don't you go spreading these lies about me or—"

"Or you'll what, Wingate?" Doyle asked from the stall's doorway.

And Leigh nearly collapsed with relief. "Doyle!"

Trying to make it look as if he were tired of the game, Keith backed off. "I see you brought your goon along."

"All women could use protection from you, Wingate."

Ignoring Doyle's taunt, Keith gave Leigh one of his most sincere smiles. "I'm deeply hurt that you don't trust me."

"I rarely have to be taught the same lesson twice." No way was she about to admit the truth—that Doyle had shown up out of nowhere to save her for the second time in two days. Instead she attacked again. "You never answered me, Keith." She shot a guilty look toward Doyle. "Did you drug High Flyer?" And was aware of Doyle's immediate scowl.

"I didn't answer, did I?" Keith seemed to think about it. "All right. Since you went through all this trouble to see me, that's the least I can do." He drew the moment out, making her want to pummel him. "No, I did not drug your colt, although I can't exactly say that I'm sorry someone else chose to do so."

"A man died," she reminded him.

"So he did." Keith shrugged carelessly and shouldered past Doyle. Once in the aisle, he said, "Now, get off my property, both of you. And, Ashleigh, honey, if you so much as repeat this accusation to one other person . . . I'll sue you for every penny you have, including your third of the farm."

His promise took away Leigh's breath long enough for him to make a clean escape. Was suing her for her share of the farm part of his plan? Or had it been a spontaneous threat?

Then she realized Doyle was staring at her in a none-too-friendly way.

Leigh avoided his eyes as she pushed past him and into the aisle. "We'd better get out of here." She waited until they were outside the barn before saying, more lightly than she was feeling, "Seems like you have the knack for knowing when to show up."

"Save the flattery." Doyle's expression was grim. "What in the world were you thinking of to come here and face Wingate alone?"

"I thought I could get at the truth." She knew she sounded defensive. "We were married."

"And he was always truthful with you then. Right?"

"No, but I knew how to get to him. I still do."

"So you believed him when he said he didn't drug High Flyer?"

"It felt like the truth, but I'm not sure," she admitted. "Maybe if you hadn't shown when you did, I might have gotten more out of him."

"Or he just might have pummeled you into that wall."

Ignoring the obvious, she said, "I suppose Oakes told you where to find me."

As they turned toward the parking lot, he said, "No. I followed you."

That gave her pause. "You *what?*"

"When you put me off about going back to the track this afternoon, I knew you were up to something. So I raced over to the farm and waited for you to leave."

Not breaking stride, she glared at him. "Doyle McCoy, how dare you skulk around and track me like I'm some kind of a criminal."

"How dare you go off on your own without discussing it with me first," he returned harshly. "I thought we were supposed to be partners here."

"We are. This was just something I had to do myself." That was it—Leigh didn't plan on justifying her actions any further.

As if he sensed her determination, Doyle dropped the subject. "We can go to the track now. Maybe get Lamar to do some fancy talking."

He wanted to see the bookie again! The thirty thousand must be eating a hole in his pocket. The very thought of Doyle placing more bets in the name of getting information out of the bookie made Leigh ill.

"No!" she said sharply. "That is, *I* can't. One of my mares is going into labor." Which was true. "Summer's Breeze hasn't eaten since yesterday and she was real restless all morning. She had some problems last year—didn't want to nurse her foal. I've got to check on her before I do anything."

"I might as well join you, then," Doyle said. "To keep you out of trouble."

Leigh was pleasantly surprised. And relieved. Though nothing would necessarily keep Doyle from getting to the track later. Or the next day.

They headed back for Wind Racer in their separate vehicles and parked near the main broodmare barn. A pair of box stalls had been set aside for foaling and were lined with clean long-stemmed rye straw that was free of dust and mold. Summer's Breeze had occupied one of the stalls since midmorning and, according to Leigh's assistant, Penny, had never stopped pacing and had rolled several times.

"If you hadn't of come back soon, I was going to call the vet," Penny said.

"I'll take over. You start rounding up the other mares and foals." If she got tied up, it would take Penny twice as long to do the work of two, so she might as well start early.

Doyle was watching Summer's Breeze. "She's rolling again. Are you sure she doesn't have colic?"

"No, it's the labor." The mare awkwardly rose, stomped her hind feet and made a kicking motion toward her belly. "It's not unusual, just not comfortable to watch."

"Not comfortable for her, either. How long do you expect this to go on?"

"Hard to tell," Leigh said honestly. "She could go into the next stage of labor at any time or she could keep this up for as long as a full day."

"So if we're in for the long haul, we might as well be comfortable." Doyle checked out the stall across the aisle, which was also set up for foaling. It was empty. "How about I get a blanket and a picnic dinner and we can bunk down to wait in here?"

"Sounds good," said Leigh, grateful he was being so understanding. "I'd rather not go too far away until after the foal is born."

While Doyle left to take care of dinner, Leigh helped Penny get the mares and foals settled, checking on Summer's Breeze every ten minutes or so.

And when he returned an hour later, Doyle dropped off the supplies in the empty stall, then pitched in to wind things up. Afterward, Leigh told Penny she could leave, but asked her to come back extra-early the next morning. Again, she checked on the mother-to-be.

"How's it going, Breezy?" Leigh cooed to the mare who eyed her balefully. No change. She sighed. "Hang in there." The encouragement was as much for herself as for the horse. "Pretty soon the discomfort will be over, and you'll have a nice new foal to mother."

Doyle was in the other stall, mounding hay in a pile against the wall. "Hungry?"

"Anxious." Leigh helped him build a comfortable seating area. She could volunteer to get chairs, but this was so much more inviting. "I always worry until the foal is born and I'm sure everyone is all right."

"Sounds like a lot of worrying."

"And about a month's worth of nights with little or no sleep. Not all in a row, thank goodness."

They spread a plaid blanket over the hay and sat next to each other, comfortably close. Leigh could see directly across the aisle into the mare's stall.

Doyle pulled out a bottle of wine and a plastic glass for her, a can of beer for himself. "We can steady our nerves while we wait."

Leigh laughed, but a few sips later she was indeed more relaxed and able to get at least part of her mind off the pacing going on across the aisle.

"So, what do you really think, Doyle?" she asked, staring down at the Chablis in her plastic glass. "Are we going to figure out who drugged High Flyer? Or are we spinning our wheels, asking for more trouble?"

"If only Carl Janks would remember who wore a gold horseshoe for luck, we just might put everything together." Doyle took a swig of beer. "How many suspects do we really have? If you eliminate Keith, that leaves only Harley, and I know you don't want to think he did it."

"I didn't say I eliminated Keith, though when I was with him the only thing he considered good luck was his looks," Leigh said bitterly.

She couldn't for the life of her figure out who else might have a reason to taint the farm's reputation—and she was nearly certain that was the motive. Wouldn't it be ironic if the answers were under her nose and she couldn't see them.

"Someone with Wingate's money probably wouldn't get his hands dirty, not when he could pay someone else," Doyle said.

That brought to mind the bit of conversation she'd overheard. "Claude was trying to get money out of Keith today. I don't know for what. To tell the truth, I was wondering if he wasn't demanding hush money."

Digging into the paper sack, Doyle paused. "Blackmail? Claude?"

"You know, the wake wasn't the only time Claude was sneaking around someplace."

"When else?"

"Right before the race. I'd checked on High Flyer and had mud on my shoes. I was going around the barn looking for something to clean them with...and I heard Desiree ask Claude what he was doing back there. I couldn't hear his explanation, and I guess I didn't think anything of it."

"So Claude was on the backside before the Blue Grass," Doyle said thoughtfully. "As well as Lamar Graspin."

"A conspiracy of some kind?"

Doyle shrugged. "Let's eat. We need brain food." But no sooner had he spooned his potato and bean salads onto his paper plate than he said, "Only one problem with Claude's being mixed up in this. Pop. He's Claude's best friend. Claude wouldn't set him up to take the fall."

Leigh swallowed a bite of sandwich. "What if someone else set up Oakes—Lamar, maybe—and Claude didn't know about it?"

"I just find it hard to believe Claude was in on some kind of conspiracy. Maybe he saw something he wasn't meant to and is trying to blackmail Keith. You didn't get any idea of what he wanted the money for?"

She shook her head and helped herself to the salads. "I was trying to lead up to the money issue with small talk. Claude got real defensive. Said I should look to my own family and then point a finger."

"I know you won't like this," Doyle said, "but he could have meant Vanessa."

"You're right, I don't like it. Mama would never knowingly hurt a person or an animal. And she would never do anything illegal!"

"But would she cover for someone who did? Harley?"

Leigh hadn't thought of that. "Oh, God, I hope not!"

A solution seemed impossible to reach without more knowledge. They could go around and around forever and not have a conclusive answer. Though she felt like telling him that if her mother could be suspect so could his father, Leigh concentrated on eating, until a whinny from the opposite stall reminded her of why she was there in the first place. Setting her plate down on the blanket, she rushed to check on Summer's Breeze. Doyle followed on her heels.

"Shouldn't be long now before she goes down for the count." Leigh noted the sweat on the mare's shoulder, flanks and chest. "Would you call Doc Halpern?" she asked, indicating the telephone on a nearby wall. "Number's posted."

"Vet's at Bluegrass Acres delivering another foal," Doyle called a few moments later. "His wife wants to know if she should send him right over afterward."

"It'll be too late, if we're lucky." Leigh tried not to worry. "Yeah, have her send him over." He would need to check over the foal in any case.

When Summer's Breeze's water broke, Leigh checked her watch. If she couldn't see the foal after ten minutes or so of hard labor, she would call Doc Halpern at Bluegrass Acres herself.

She needn't have worried. Eight minutes into the labor, she saw the front feet of the foal.

"It's coming!" she cried.

Sitting at the mare's head, where he'd been stroking her and talking to her in a soft voice, Doyle scooted closer to Leigh to take a look. "Should we do anything?"

"Not until we see the nose."

Leigh readied herself and, as the forelegs slid out, she gently held the foal's ankles. It wasn't until the nose appeared tucked onto the knees that she exerted a slight downward pressure.

"We don't have to pull unless the mare is having problems," she explained.

The wet body slid out of the mare easily, however, and Leigh felt an even greater rush than she usually did at this moment—all because Doyle was sharing it with her. She let go of the foal when only the tiny back feet remained inside.

"They're resting," she said, leaning back near Doyle.

He gathered her close. "Congratulations," he murmured, his lips near her ear. When she faced him, he kissed the smile from her mouth and filled her with a different kind of pleasure. Pleasure of a far more per-

sonal nature. A bevy of soft kisses trailed along her
cheek and up to her brow before Doyle settled his
forehead against hers.

They remained snuggled together, content for a moment, until the foal finally slid free of its mother. Leigh
moved forward to check that the perfect-looking little
colt was breathing. Then she pressed her thumb and
forefinger down over the top of his nostrils toward the
muzzle to clear out the mucus. And finally she checked
to make certain the foal's mouth was free of foreign
material so that he could breathe properly.

When she glanced back at Doyle, she was beaming.
"Everything seems perfect."

"So, do I hand out cigars or what?" he asked,
sounding exactly as a proud new father might.

Leigh sat back on her haunches and grinned. "Ap-
ples would be more appropriate, don't you think?"
She'd never felt so content in her life. Surely this was
the way a relationship was meant to be—sharing special moments.

Within minutes, the foal was thrashing and the mare
was rising to her feet, severing the umbilical cord. Just
about the time Doc Halpern arrived to take over. He
checked the foal and treated the navel stump, then examined Summer's Breeze. With an assurance that everything was as it should be, he was on his way back
home.

But Leigh's work wasn't done yet. "I still can't
leave," she told Doyle as she watered and fed Summer's Breeze. "I have to wait for the mare to pass the
afterbirth and to make certain the foal starts nursing
within a couple of hours."

"Then we might as well get comfortable again. And finish our dinner."

She'd forgotten about eating, but suddenly she was ravenous. Returning to the other stall, they finished every bit of the food Doyle had brought, after which she settled back into his arms. "I needed this. The quiet. The caring."

In tune with her thoughts, he shifted so he was over her and could stare deep into her eyes. She ran a hand through the chestnut hair drooping over his forehead and left a rabbit ridge that made him look kind of silly. Smiling up at him, she thought he might kiss her, *wanted* him to kiss her.

His eyes burned, telling her he wanted that, too.

But he didn't move as her fingers explored the face that reflected the rough kind of life he'd lived. No smooth edges, but signs of inner character—like the nose that had been broken when he'd saved that colt and had won her love the first time around.

That was the *real* Doyle, the one beneath the surface of the crass handicapper she'd thought of him as for so long.

The one she wanted to get to know more intimately.

As if he sensed that, he kissed her. Slowly. Allowing passion to build. She shifted under him. Restless. Wanting. He gave. Stroking her through her clothes with hands as sure and strong as he himself. He mounted her, a tiny rocking movement wedging him between her legs. Through two pairs of jeans, she felt a need that was as great as her own. Shuddering, she moved her hips appreciatively.

She had a moment's pause, wondered whether what they were agreeing to here was right. Whether it would last. Whether he could feel about her the way she did about him.

He insinuated a hand up under her T-shirt, turning her skin to gooseflesh.

"You feel so good," Doyle groaned, finding a breast and freeing it from the light sport bra she wore.

They were from different sides of the racetrack—his words, not hers. And she wasn't certain that he could overcome a childhood prejudice and become part of her world as she was already part of his.

Leigh didn't want to think about Doyle's betting problem. The issue was too complicated, too fraught with traps to consider now. Besides, their coming together would be the biggest gamble of all.

And as he worked her nipple until it tightened, until she grew achy inside, she dashed the mental obstacles and began removing the tangible ones. His shirt. Her T-shirt. Without speaking, he rolled off of her so they could shed the rest.

When he was naked, Doyle settled on his back, took her ponytail in his hand and gently pulled her on top.

Thighs tightening around his hips, she urged him to move boldly and fast. Then she rode him hard until they crossed the finish line in a dead heat. Together.

Chapter Eleven

When their bodies had cooled and their minds had cleared, Doyle sacrificed his romantic instincts for a moment to be practical. "We'd better get some clothes on or we'll be scratching ourselves to death."

Leigh didn't need convincing to pull on her clothes, but before she could get back into her T-shirt, Doyle stopped her.

"Some bruise," he said, inspecting her shoulder and wishing he could kiss the hurt away. "You got this from the tussle with Wind Tunnel?"

Nodding, Leigh said, "That and the one on my hip." She checked the fleshy part of her upper arm. "The new one with teeth marks is a present from Typhoon. My, he's got an ugly disposition, not unlike Wind Tunnel."

There was an edge to her voice, and she was frowning, making Doyle wonder what was going on inside her pretty head.

"They *are* related, right?"

"Right." She frowned harder.

"What?"

"Probably nothing."

"It doesn't look like nothing."

"*Look*...that's it," Leigh said as if she'd just had a revelation. She finished pulling on her T-shirt. "Tomorrow morning, I want to look at some videotapes."

"Of what?"

She popped up to her feet. "Races." And crossed the aisle to check on the mare and foal. "How you doing, Breezy?"

Doyle told himself that he should not take offense just because she hadn't offered him some soft words before turning her attention to the horses. The animals were, after all, her responsibility, and he and Leigh *had* gotten carried away physically at an inopportune time. So he joined her, feeling a rush of tenderness as he watched the wobbly legged colt explore the stall while his dam inspected him.

Keeping her attention on the horses, Leigh cooed, "And you, little guy, how come you're not interested in your mama's milk, huh?"

"Hmm, maybe we were distracted and missed something," Doyle suggested.

"We weren't preoccupied *that* long."

"Not my fault. You were the one in a hurry," he teased, slipping an arm around her waist.

While she didn't shrug away, neither did she snuggle into the shelter of his body as Doyle might have liked. He told himself that didn't mean anything and tried to content himself with touching her.

"At least Summer's Breeze is interested in him," Leigh was saying. "He's only her second foal. Last time, she was so afraid, I had to distract her to keep her still while Penny encouraged the little filly to nurse. I think she's ready for anything this time, thank goodness."

"You know, the foal imitates High Flyer."

"He is a miniature of my Bad Boy, isn't he? Of course, they're both descended from Fly Like the Wind."

Doyle heard the edge to her voice again, but he figured if Leigh wanted him to know what she was thinking, she would tell him.

The next hour was split between small talk and checking on the mare and her foal. He sensed Leigh's relief when the colt finally realized he was hungry and found his mother's teat. Not much later, Summer's Breeze passed the afterbirth and Leigh took care of the situation, turning down his offer of help. By the time she declared herself done for the day, it was near midnight. She was looking exhausted but wide-eyed, as if her mind didn't intend to let her body rest.

"Come on over here and relax," he coaxed, knowing she needed a good sleep—something she wouldn't find, wired as she was. Besides, he wanted to recapture that feeling of closeness that was rapidly becoming a memory. "Have another glass of wine. You'll sleep better if you do."

"You don't have to twist my tail to convince me."

She plopped down next to him on the blanket and Doyle poured her a full glass, which she eyed with suspicion. "Trying to get me drunk so you can take advantage of me?"

"Only if I can do it while you're sleeping."

"Could make for some mighty interesting dreams," she murmured.

Taking a sip of wine, she leaned back and slipped into the curve of his arm. Doyle found himself breathing easier. Almost forgetting there were reasons why they shouldn't have gotten so close.

"You've made me think about something," Leigh said. "You seem to enjoy the horses as much as you did when you were a teenager. And you're really good with them, Doyle. So why pick a career where you write about horses rather than work with them?"

"Money." He was reminded of the primary difference between them, the thing that troubled him most. "I didn't have enough to be an owner/breeder." He could afford to own a few horses now, of course, and maybe even a small farm, if not the kind of operation she was used to. "And I didn't have enough talent to be a trainer. What was left—a job on the backside? Being a groom like Pop wasn't exactly something I wanted to do for the rest of my life."

"But being a handicapper was?"

"Let's say I used the talent I had with numbers to my best advantage."

Leigh seemed to withdraw a tad, and Doyle figured she was thinking about his betting again. Why couldn't she believe he had that situation under control?

"Betting on horses is something I'm good at. It's never been a problem to anyone but Susan."

"Is that why you tried to quit?"

"I did quit."

Admittedly, he could be tempted, especially with his "accidental" winnings from Lamar Graspin, but he wasn't willing to gamble away a life again. Not that he exactly had one. He'd been alone since Susan had left him. He'd had women, of course, just not one he'd taken a shine to like Leigh. He didn't doubt that his betting would be a problem to her, too...if he chose to do so...which he didn't. She was blowing everything out of proportion.

"I don't want to get into an argument and spoil one of the nicest nights of my life," she told him, setting down her empty glass and curling her body against his, "but I wish you would do some real hard thinking for your own sake. You've been splitting hairs about this gambling thing."

"That's your opinion."

"Yes, it is only my opinion," she quickly continued. "But I think that if you'd been able to control what you refer to as a talent, you would be with Susan and your children now instead of with me. You didn't even try to prove her wrong until after she left you."

"I didn't have to prove anything to her."

"Then I guess you feel you have only yourself to answer to," she said, sounding sad. "Keith had the same attitude."

"He was fooling around with other women. That's a whole different game."

"Different addiction," she corrected. "Only you know deep in your heart whether or not betting on the ponies is *your* addiction. And if it is, you have to admit it before you can truly control it."

"I'm not—"

She slipped her hand over his mouth. "Shh, no arguments, okay? I'm done. I wish *I* were your addiction. Please, think about that."

Though Doyle didn't say that he would, how could he help but think about it once she'd brought up the subject? Leigh relaxed against his chest, and the hand that had shushed him curled around his neck, sending longing coursing through him. Almost immediately, her breathing deepened. Doyle crouched down a bit to absorb her weight more comfortably, not wanting to disturb her.

She was asleep.

And he was left wide-awake with the certainty that he didn't have room for two addictions in his life...not if he wanted her to be one of them.

"Yoo-hoo, Leigh, I'm back."

Waking with a start, Leigh blinked the sleep from her mind and turned to see Penny watching with amusement. Daylight streamed into the stall where she and Doyle had spent the night in each other's arms. She tried to disentangle without waking him, but to no avail.

"Morning," he grumbled.

His smile was lazy and suggestive, driving Leigh to her feet. "Penny's here. And we have work to do."

"Give me a minute and I'll help. If ever I wake up this arm and get it functioning," he muttered, shaking the limb she'd been lying on.

"Sorry," Penny whispered. Then she said, "I've already checked on Summer's Breeze and the foal. They're both looking good. I gave her some more wet bran mash."

Anxious whinnies from other stalls made Leigh laugh. "And made a few ladies jealous she got special treatment. Let's get this brood fed."

Again Doyle pitched in and helped. Again Leigh thought it a shame he couldn't be doing something more satisfying than manipulating numbers for a living. She wondered if he'd thought at all about the addiction thing, or if he'd forgotten it as quickly as she'd dropped off in his arms. If he couldn't even admit gambling was a problem, how could he deal with the myriad other conflicts that would come up in a relationship?

If she wanted a relationship with him, that was.

Watching him work with the horses, seeing the personal way he dealt with them as only someone who really cared about animals could, she knew she wanted. Oh, how she wanted. Keith had been concerned and firm but had kept the horses at a distance the way he'd done with her. Like all creatures, horses responded to what was offered. Any horse would prefer Doyle to Keith. As would any woman in her right mind.

But until the addiction issue was settled for her—and the frontside/backside conflict for him—perhaps they ought to cool things down a bit. And so, after the mares and their offspring were fed, watered and pastured, and Penny was off mixing a batch of feed with vitamins and minerals, Leigh circumvented Doyle's advances.

"Let's take a look at those videotapes I mentioned, then get the breakfast Mama's making for us." She'd called the house a while ago and asked her mother to make it a big one.

"You want to watch old races before we eat?" Doyle complained. But he followed her back to the house and into the foyer without making a big production of the decision. Though before they entered the study, which Leigh and her mother used as the official farm office, he couldn't help but point out, "Smells like Vanessa's cooking up a storm. My mouth's watering."

"That you, Ashleigh?" Mama called from the kitchen.

"We'll be there in a while," Leigh yelled in return. She pushed Doyle inside and closed the door. Her stomach churning with emotion rather than hunger, she walked over to a shelved wall and pulled two videotapes from the substantial collection of races. "If I'm right..."

"Right about what?"

"You'll see."

Wanting Doyle to form his own conclusions, Leigh didn't explain. Maybe her instincts were askew and she would be alone in her uneasy suspicions. Praying that she would indeed be proved wrong, that the unthinkable had not, after all, occurred, she popped a cassette into the recorder. Whatever the outcome, she had to know for certain.

"This first race took place last year," she told him, picking up the remote. She hoped her voice was steady, free of emotion that would give it away.

As soon as the picture steadied, Doyle murmured, "High Flyer and Typhoon," and pulled a nearby high-backed leather chair closer to the television.

"Watch." Leigh perched on the chair's arm as High Flyer went easily into starting gate four. Two other horses were led into their chutes. Then Typhoon.

"They're pushing him," Doyle noted. "Though that's not anything unusual." A moment later, he was a bit more indignant. "Look at that! Typhoon tried to nip one of the handlers the way he did you."

One last horse was loaded and the bell tolled. Both colts started fast and maintained solid positions in the middle of the field until halfway through the second turn. Both fired, one after the other. High Flyer focused straight ahead on the finish line, but Typhoon had a way of hanging his head low and cocking it slightly to glance at any horse coming up beside him too quickly.

"Wait a minute," Doyle said. "Did he just try to nip High Flyer?"

Leigh nodded and used the remote to replay the action in slow motion. "Exactly what Desiree said she thought he was planning on doing in the Blue Grass."

"You already have a tape of the Blue Grass?" Doyle asked.

"No."

She ejected the videotape and traded it for the second one.

The quality of the old footage revealed the age of the race. Resolution and color were poor compared to modern standards. But the horse in question was instantly recognizable because his size and color and marking were identical to Typhoon's. Leigh glanced at Doyle, who gave her a curious expression before they both settled to watch. She held her breath as horses were loaded into the starting gate.

"Wind Tunnel," he murmured.

Leigh remained silent as handlers pushed Wind Tunnel into his slot. The bay turned and tried to nip one of them.

Doyle sat forward. "Exactly like Typhoon."

The race started. Wind Tunnel stayed to the middle of the field, fired at the second turn, then, head hung low, cocked it to glance at a horse coming up alongside him. Leigh pressed a button on the remote and the on-screen action slowed. Wind Tunnel's head turned. He bared his teeth ever so slightly before the jockey used a crop on him and made him concentrate on business.

"Like Typhoon," Doyle repeated, the words sounding hollow.

And though he fell silent, Leigh was convinced they'd drawn the same conclusion. They stared at each other without speaking for a moment, and she knew he didn't want to put words to what she didn't want to believe. Her eyes filled with tears and her throat closed tight.

And Mama chose exactly that moment to barge into the office to announce, "Breakfast will surely be cold if you don't get into the kitchen."

Her smile faded as she studied first their serious faces, then the television. Leigh glanced at the screen to see Wind Tunnel cross the finish line in slow motion. She froze the image and turned back to her mother, who had gone still and pale.

"Fly Like the Wind isn't Typhoon's granddaddy, is he?" Leigh asked. "It's Wind Tunnel. What does it mean, Mama?"

"It doesn't mean anything. Come eat."

"Time for the truth."

Her mother started to leave. Leigh flung herself in front of the door. Mama's hands fluttered, and she shook her head. Leigh refused to break eye contact.

In the space of a heartbeat, the face that looked so like her own aged a dozen years. And in that second, Leigh's heart broke, because she knew she couldn't let the lie go on. Other people were involved—and the lineage of who-knew-how-many thoroughbreds. Her mother would be ruined. Wind Racer would be ruined. And she would be the one to do it, Leigh realized. The one to kill her father's dream.

"What did you and Daddy do?" she whispered.

"Not him," Mama finally choked out. "He never knew."

Leigh wanted to plead with her to take the words back. Instead, she demanded, "Tell me."

"Your daddy was critically ill for so very long! The insurance ran out. Then our savings. I wanted to sell the farm, but Charles said that was not an option. He would do without treatment, but he would not do without his dream. Was I to deprive a sick man of the one thing he loved more than anythin'?"

"He had us."

"But this farm and its future was his addiction. Charles said he would rather die than sell the place. I got a loan to keep us going. We won some good purses and things were lookin' up. Then broodmares covered by Fly Like the Wind stopped taking. Some kind of sterility problem. The farm was dependent on his stud fees. The way things had been goin', I was afraid we were about to lose everything."

Those stud fees had been very high for the time, Leigh knew, because Fly Like the Wind had won the Kentucky Derby. She could well believe the farm's mortgage and expenses had been paid for by that one stallion.

"So you pulled a switch, using a horse who could never bring in anywhere near the same money." Leigh had been willing to face it happening once. She hadn't imagined how many foals might be involved.

"Fly Like the Wind and Wind Tunnel were full brothers," her mother was saying somewhat defensively. "They had the same genes. It wasn't like we were cheatin' anyone by using some claimer."

Surely her mother couldn't believe that it made a difference if the horse were a graded stakes winner or a cheap claimer. "We *who?*" Leigh asked.

"Me, I'm the one."

"You couldn't have done it alone physically."

"Ashleigh, let me out of here. Now."

"No, Mama, not until I have the whole truth."

Her mother's will surfaced for a moment, but when Leigh refused to move from the door, Mama said, "They were only acting on my orders. I can't betray them."

Leigh remembered Thane telling her Harley had always been loyal to her family... they must both have been in on this. "Thane, Harley and who else?"

Her mother gave Doyle a panicked look before staring down at her hands.

"Not Pop..." Doyle's words were a shocked whisper.

Her mother's lips trembled but she pursed them together, obviously unwilling to confirm the truth. At the time, Thane had been stallion manager, Harley an up-and-coming trainer and Oakes a trusted groom. Leigh touched Doyle's arm and, without taking his eyes off her mother, covered her hand with his. He was affected by this, too.

"I did what I had to," her mother went on, her voice suddenly steely. "Then we won some Grade I stakes races and I could stop. I retired Fly Like the Wind from stud as soon as I could, at the end of that one season."

As if that had been the end of it! "Mama, what happened at the Blue Grass..."

"My fault." Mama's face crumpled, and tears sprang from her eyes. "All my fault. But where was I goin' to get more money? I've practically bankrupted the farm."

"No wonder you didn't let me at the books!"

"The demands kept comin'. And now Jimmy Diaz is dead. A man is dead, and all I wanted to do was take care of my family."

"Someone was blackmailing you?" Doyle asked.

Mama nodded and crossed to the desk that was old and solid and had been there forever. Reaching under the center drawer, she did something that made a popping sound. A lock releasing. A narrow portion of the facing above the row of drawers on the right freed itself of the design. A secret drawer that Leigh hadn't known about. But then, she hadn't known a lot of things. Her mother removed a folded piece of paper and handed it to Leigh.

Textured, wheat-colored stationery.

"Identical to the paper I found with the threat to Jimmy," Leigh said, looking at Doyle. "Whoever has been blackmailing Mama sent that one, too."

Reluctantly, she unfolded it.

Vanessa—
You were warned. Unless you come up with the money owed, you won't have a Kentucky Derby entry...

It was, of course, unsigned.

As Doyle stepped forward to take it from her, Leigh said, "My God, it sounds like the blackmailer's intent was to kill High Flyer. Mama, when did you get this?"

"The morning of the Blue Grass. I was understandably upset—the reason I didn't go with you. But in the end, I had to see for myself."

No wonder her mother blamed herself. She'd known something was going to happen but had been powerless to stop it. Doyle handed the note back to Leigh. She read it once more as if the few lines could give up its secrets and tell her who wrote them. A foolish hope. Leigh refolded it and set it in the hidden drawer, which she then shut. Examining the desk, she had difficulty finding the hidden edges, even though she now knew the drawer existed.

"Mama, you keep this locked up and don't let anyone know anything about it until we have need for it." From her mother's expression, Leigh determined her warning came too late. "Who knows? Harley?" She didn't really need to ask. She could see it was so on her mother's face. Hurt, Leigh whispered, "You told Harley Barnett but you didn't tell me, your own daughter?"

"I had to tell him. I owe him that much. This whole thing could destroy his career."

"But he could be the one who sent it," Doyle pointed out.

"No, Harley's loyal!" Mama insisted. "He would never do that to me."

Though she didn't agree, Leigh didn't argue the point. She gave her mother a brief hug—all she could manage at the moment. She needed time to digest what she had learned before she could offer sympathy or assurances.

Her whole world was collapsing around her.

They spent a few minutes on breakfast. The food was cold and seemed tasteless, but Leigh ate because she knew it was necessary. Interaction was limited to passing plates, giving her time to think about her mother's elaborate charade. No matter that her intentions had been good, she'd been misguided. Criminal. Doubting that Mama could come up with such a plan herself, Leigh wondered if Harley hadn't done it for her.

Or Oakes.

Leigh kept her peace until she and Doyle left the kitchen for the yard. She headed straight for the farm truck. "We have to see your father again."

"Pop?" Doyle caught her arm and stopped her. "What for?"

She shrugged out of his grip and kept going. "Because he knows far more than he told us."

"You suspect him, even though he was set up?"

"If he didn't write that note to Jimmy himself," Leigh said, remembering how it had disappeared from her purse the same way Oakes claimed the note to him had vanished. She climbed into the driver's seat and started the engine. "Maybe the other note, the one Oakes couldn't find, was a convenient cover story. Are you coming?"

Doyle knew she was going with or without him. He quickly rounded the truck and threw himself into the passenger side. Not softening his anger, he bellowed, "You really think Pop's capable of blackmail, drugging a horse and hurting you?"

She shrank from his hostile expression, so unlike the mocking facade he used to wear around her. "No, but I also never thought Mama was capable of taking people's money under false pretenses."

"We're talking two different things here," Doyle continued heatedly. "Vanessa didn't mean to hurt anyone. Whoever left you in the pasture with Wind Tunnel *did!*"

He fumed in silence for a moment, and Leigh drove off, leaving the farm and her personal burgeoning nightmare behind. He was right—the two situations *were* different. But if they were to get to the truth, they couldn't close their minds to any possibility.

As she turned onto the pike and headed for Wingate Stud, Doyle said, "What I would like to know is how Vanessa could have made the switch between horses for an entire breeding season without your ever guessing." Though he still sounded tense, he was no longer shouting.

Leigh counted back to the year it all happened, right before Fly Like the Wind was retired from stud. "I simply wasn't there. In the spring, I was finishing my last year of college, and then Mama insisted I take the grand tour of Europe with Harmony and Jennifer as planned. I was gone half the summer. I never realized..."

She couldn't go on. What kind of a daughter was she not to have realized the desperate financial circumstances her parents had been in? What kind of a daughter would consider turning in her own mother?

The question was still eating at her as she swung onto the Wingate Stud property. Leaving the farm truck in the parking lot, they asked the nearest employee about Oakes's whereabouts and were directed to one of the smaller barns. Expecting to see Keith at any moment, Leigh held her breath until they arrived and found Oakes inside alone.

Doyle's gut was tied in a knot. If he'd felt bad the day they'd questioned his father at Keeneland, today he felt worse. He didn't believe Pop would have anything to do with blackmail or drugging or mugging.

But he had to ask.

"Pop," he called as he strode toward the work area where Oakes was paging through a feed list tacked to the wall. "We have to talk to you."

His father seemed more resigned than startled to see the two of them approaching together, as if he could guess their purpose, though no doubt he figured they were here to ask him about Jimmy again. The pages of the list flipped through his fingers, and he turned to face them. And waited.

Doyle hated this, resented Leigh for making him do it. He also knew that if Vanessa hadn't entered the study when she had, he would have expected Leigh to seek out her mother and confront her the same way.

He took a deep breath and went directly to the past. "We know about the switch, Pop. Wind Tunnel being substituted for Fly Like the Wind. Vanessa admitted everything." If only his father would deny being involved.

But Oakes nodded. "I helped."

"If you were in on it," Leigh said, "then why have you been blackmailing Mama?"

The question popped out of her so fast that Doyle didn't have a chance to stop it.

"Blackmail?" his father echoed, sounding properly horrified. He ignored Leigh and stared at Doyle. "Someone's blackmailing Vanessa…and you think it's me?"

"I don't think so, Pop, and I'm sure Ash doesn't either—"

"Don't speak for me. I have a mouth."

"Yeah, a big one."

Oakes McCoy straightened his back and faced his accuser. "I'm not blackmailing your mama. I would never do such a thing. I *couldn't* do such a thing."

"Why should I believe you?" Leigh demanded.

"Because of the way I feel about her."

"What? Are you going to tell me you have some loyalty to the Scotts even though you've been working for Wingate Stud for all these years?"

"I always admired your mama, Ashleigh. But when your daddy took sick and Vanessa worked so hard to keep the farm going for him, to give him something to live for, I fell in love with her. I left Wind Racer to work for Mr. Wingate because I couldn't stand watching them together anymore." He sighed, his shoulders slumping. "I felt so bad about your daddy and all, and I couldn't stand being so close to Vanessa day after day, knowing all her feelings were for him."

Whatever Doyle had expected his father to say, it hadn't been this. His shock was reflected in Leigh's expression.

"You'd think we'd know our own parents a whole lot better," he muttered.

Oakes shook his head. "So, after all this time, someone's digging up the past. Other than Vanessa, only three of us knew. Four if you count Edgar Dalton," he said, referring to the vet who'd died a few years earlier. "I can't feature Thane or Harley turning on Vanessa, either."

"I wouldn't trust Harley further than I could throw him," Doyle stated.

"Are you sure no one else could have known?" Leigh asked.

"We were real careful, did the covering after midnight. Took turns being on watch. I suppose someone could have seen and never said. Or could have found out if Thane or Harley or Edgar spilled his guts over a coupla beers. But why wait all these years to do something about it?"

"The question of the century," Doyle said. Now that the situation was out in the open, he couldn't see any reason to keep anything from his father. "Pop, whoever is blackmailing Vanessa is the same person who sent those notes to you and Jimmy. Stationery's the same." He ignored the choking sound coming from Leigh.

"What are you saying, son? That Jimmy's death had something to do with our switching stallions?"

"Time for us to leave," Leigh suggested, giving Doyle an intense look.

"Time for the truth." Doyle could tell she didn't like it from the tightening of her lips, but she backed off. "Leigh and I keep arguing about who drugged High Flyer and why. But I've got something that might point us in the right direction. We found it in the colt's stall after the accident." He pulled out his wallet and slipped the gold charm from its hiding place. "Ever see this before?"

Taking the worn bit of gold and squinting at it, Oakes turned ashen. "Couldn't be."

"Who?" Leigh asked. "Who does it belong to?"

"I could be wrong—it's been years since I seen it."

Doyle felt a rush of adrenaline kick in. "Years or not, Pop, who do you think it belongs to?"

"If he was wearing it that day, it sure as hell didn't do him much good." Oakes shook his head. His expression grave, he said, "Claude Walker."

Chapter Twelve

"Claude Walker?" Leigh echoed. "I suspected he knew something, but if he lost that good-luck piece in High Flyer's stall, he had to have been involved."

Oakes protested. "Claude would never get himself involved in fixing a race."

Doyle took the charm from his father. He had a difficult time believing it, too, but he was staring at the proof. "Are you certain he wasn't desperate for money?"

"His girl paid off the mortgage on their farm, and Claude gets disability and a pension from the Disabled Jockeys Fund. That's more than enough for him to live on."

"Sometimes enough *isn't* enough," Leigh said.

"I don't care what you two say—I know the man," Oakes growled. "He's been my best friend for years. Claude would never do anything to hurt a horse, and especially not another jockey. Do you think he'd chance being responsible for someone else ending up crippled?"

Pop was making sense. "You might be right," Doyle reluctantly admitted.

"What?" Leigh cried.

Doyle tried to pacify her. "You could be right, too. You thought Claude might be hitting on Wingate. Could be you're on the nose about that. Maybe Wingate learned about the stallion switching when he was married to you."

"And not say anything?"

"Why would he unless it was in his best interests?" Doyle was getting into his new theory. "He didn't want to threaten the good of the farm then. But your divorcing him changed things. You told me he's trying to destroy you economically, and Vanessa admitted the farm's practically bankrupt."

Leigh nodded. "And Keith would see drugging High Flyer as another warning to pay up—like the mares being turned loose on the pike and the stallion getting hold of bad feed."

"But he wasn't careful enough. He had a witness. Claude."

"Then how did the horseshoe end up in the stall?" Leigh asked.

"He went in looking for proof." Hearing voices immediately outside the barn, Doyle glanced over his shoulder as he speculated. "For all we know, Claude's got the syringe with Wingate's prints."

Speaking of the devil, Keith Wingate was following another groom into the barn.

"Well, well, if it isn't my dear ex-wife coming around to stir up more excitement. What's it to be today, Ashleigh, honey?"

"Don't worry, Keith, I'm not here to spite you. Doyle merely had to stop by to speak to Oakes for a minute."

"Minute's up."

Doyle turned away from Wingate and spoke to his father in a voice too low for anyone else to hear. "You won't say anything to anyone?"

For which he received a hurt glare and his father's back as Oakes returned his attention to the posted feed list.

Wingate cleared his throat officiously. "McCoy—"

"We're gone. C'mon, Ash."

Afraid she might get herself into trouble if he allowed her time to trade gibes with her ex-husband, Doyle steered her out of the barn, shouldering past Wingate without apology.

Once they hit sunlight, she pulled free of his tight grasp. "I still have all my faculties."

"Couldn't prove it by me."

"Stuff it, McCoy," she grumbled.

Doyle waited until they were halfway to the parking lot to let her temper cool before saying, "The question now is how to make Claude tell us what he knows."

"And before your father warns him."

"Pop won't do any such thing."

"Why not? He thinks his best friend is innocent and wouldn't hurt a fly."

"Because he has integrity."

"Yeah. About as much as Mama," Leigh said ruefully.

"And he loves me as much as Vanessa loves you."

She had no smart return. Doyle glanced at her. She was staring at a spot on the ground a pace in front of her feet. He couldn't blame her for being upset. She adored Vanessa, and learning that her mother wasn't the perfect person Leigh thought she was must have come as quite a shock.

When they got to the farm truck, he offered to drive, but Leigh merely glared at him and climbed in behind the wheel. And Doyle's irritation with her rose. Why did she have to be so hardheaded? He hoped she didn't treat Vanessa in the same manner. The older woman had looked as if she were about to crack from the strain.

"Vanessa needs your understanding now."

"I understand Mama fine."

The underlying edge to her voice didn't sit well with him. "Then you'll talk this thing out with her?"

"I don't want to talk about it." Leigh pulled the truck out of the lot and gunned the engine. "She did what she had to do."

"And you'll do what *you* have to do. You'll correct her mistake." When she didn't immediately agree, he asked, "Right?"

"I'm not certain," she mumbled.

"You can't cover this up."

"I don't have to turn in my own mother, either. I feel terrible about the switch, but what's done is done."

She turned onto the pike and raced for home. One glance at the speedometer told Doyle he didn't want another look.

"Ash, listen to me. People are going to find out what happened one way or the other. Wouldn't it be better if the announcement came from you?"

"What does *that* mean? That if I don't tell them, you will?" Her voice rose. "Of course. Why not? You don't have a vested interest in Wind Racer Farm."

"Is that what's most important to you? The farm?" Doyle was appalled—he hadn't expected this of her. "You're putting the future of Wind Racer before the truth?"

"We're talking about Mama."

"No, we're not. We're talking about your obsession to carry out your daddy's *addiction.*" He emphasized the last word that she had so easily applied to him but obviously didn't see as applying to herself.

"Leave Daddy out of this."

"Whether you like it or not, he's part of it. Your father's the reason Vanessa switched stallions—so that his 'dream' wouldn't die."

Leigh hit the steering wheel with the flat of her hand. "There's nothing wrong with dreams."

"There is if you let them become more important than people." Doyle wished he could make her understand that. He'd continued betting on the ponies despite Susan's objections, because in his heart he believed that someday he was going to score big, to give them all a better life. Only he hadn't wanted to believe that he'd hurt and ultimately lost his family because he *had* been addicted. Leigh had made him see that. As she'd told him, he couldn't truly control his addiction until he recognized it. The same went for her, if in a different way.

"When your father refused to sell the farm and swore he'd rather die than sell it, how do you think that made your mother feel?"

"She understood he needed something to keep him alive."

"True, but Vanessa wouldn't be human if she didn't feel like the future of Wind Racer meant more to him than she did," Doyle insisted. "And now you're determined to carry on his legacy. You married a man who was wrong for you, who didn't give you respect, no less love, because he could provide you with the means to rebuild the farm."

"I was fooled. I thought Keith and I had a common goal and that we could build a satisfying life together."

What had he expected? She had to justify her actions or she probably couldn't live with herself.

"Your thinking is all turned around, Ash. You still don't see anything wrong with your marrying Wingate, and yet you've got a major bug about my placing one lousy bet—"

She was quick to interrupt. "I don't consider a thousand dollars nothing."

"And I don't consider cheating people nothing, either! I know Vanessa well enough to be certain she agonized over what she did, not just when she was playing switch, but afterward. She had years to think about it. To remember. Your father's obsession with Wind Racer pushed her into committing a criminal act."

"But not an act that hurt anyone!"

"Does that mean you approve? Would you have done the same thing yourself?"

"You're out of line," she said coldly. "Drop it."

As they drove onto Wind Racer property, Doyle felt as if his very life were flowing out of him. There it was. Her splitting hairs when it was convenient to do so. He should have known better. She came from a class of people who put themselves above everyone else, gave themselves privileges at the expense of other people. Somehow, it always came back to the same old song. And he'd mistakenly gone back on his upbringing.

"This is really rich." He was lecturing himself as much as he was talking to her. "You were willing to sacrifice Pop when you thought he was involved. But then, he's only a groom, right? Not worthy of the same consideration, the same amount of cover-up effort as someone with blue blood."

He'd meant to make her angry and he did. Leigh screeched the truck to a halt halfway up the drive and, without a word to him, jumped out of the vehicle and ran into the house. Doyle stared after her, understanding more than he wanted to. Reaching over to the steering column, he turned the key in the ignition. As the motor died, so did his hopes for a future with Leigh in it. He traded the truck for his car and drove away, believing he would never set foot on Wind Racer land again.

After a brief encounter that would haunt him always, they had just gone back to their opposing sides of the racetrack.

LEIGH TOOK A STINGING shower that helped her swallow her fury and disappointment with Doyle faster than she might have if time weren't so critical. He could believe what he liked about his own father, but she was worried that Oakes would warn Claude and give him time to fabricate answers to some tough questions.

She was going to face Claude Walker and make him talk!

And she was going to do it alone!

Shoving thoughts of Doyle—of how much his accusations had hurt her, of how crazy in love she was with him—to the back of her mind, she dressed quickly. Barely a half hour after she'd abandoned the truck and him with it, she drove her car onto the Walkers' farm, hoping that Desiree had already left for Keeneland.

Doyle would be furious if he knew what she was up to, but she didn't care. He had no say over her actions. She did. Her mind had a will of its own and did as it liked, including thinking about Doyle when she'd forbade herself to do so. With every step she took, she felt as if he were looking over her shoulder, criticizing.

By the time she marched onto the front porch of the Walker house, Claude had wheeled himself over to the screen door.

"Ashleigh." He sounded surprised, as if he'd been expecting someone else. "Desiree's not here now."

Did he think Oakes was on his way? She had to hurry. "I didn't come to see your daughter, Claude. It's you I want to talk to."

Though his expression was suspicious—he probably figured she wanted to talk about Desiree's emotional state again—he backed away from the entrance. "Door's open."

As she passed him on her way into the living room, Leigh smelled the fumes. He'd been drinking again. A bottle of soda-pop moon sat open on the coffee table next to the telephone. The television was playing with the sound off. Had he gotten a call warning him?

"Listen, Ashleigh, if you're worried about my girl—"

"Not Desiree. You. I'm worried you've gotten yourself into an unhealthy situation."

He looked puzzled. "What situation?"

"With my ex-husband. I heard you asking him for money. Keith doesn't take to being threatened."

Claude laughed. "Threatening him? How'd you come to that? I was trying to get him to cough up a bigger donation for a Jockey Club charity. I figured he can afford it."

Leigh hadn't expected such an innocent-sounding response. She was half-convinced it was the truth.

The other half was the problem.

"If you were to ask me," she said, perching at the edge of the couch, "it sounded like you were wanting some hush money."

"Blackmail?" His good humor faded a little. "Ashleigh, you been out in the sun too long?"

"Don't think so, Claude. Either you're black-mailing Keith because *he* drugged High Flyer...or you messed with my colt yourself."

Claude's smile evaporated. "This isn't funny."

"I'm not laughing."

Neither was he. A wariness suddenly played around his eyes, and he gripped the arms of his wheelchair hard. She had to forget she'd known Claude Walker since she was a kid, had admired him as a jockey, was still friends with his daughter. If he was the one responsible for Jimmy's death, she had to know.

She had the advantage and meant to keep it. "Why weren't you at the hospital with Desiree when Jimmy died?" she asked. "And what were you doing, sneaking around the funeral home the night he was waked?"

"I don't know what you're talking about."

"I knew someone was spying on me and Desiree. Then I found the tracks your wheelchair made out on the lawn. How did you disappear on me so fast, anyway?"

Sweat started to bead his brow, and Leigh read apprehension and something else in the eyes that still met her own with a steadiness she hadn't counted on. Had she given him too little credit about the actual drugging because he was in a wheelchair? What else might he be capable of?

A thrill of fear made her go on the alert when Claude suddenly reached for the coffee table.

But all he did was pick up the recycled soda bottle. He drank straight from it. The moonshine was obviously powerful stuff. It colored Claude's chalk-white cheeks and imbued him with a renewed sense of self. He sat straighter in the wheelchair as he met her gaze.

"I'll be askin' you to leave now."

Leigh shook her head. "Sorry. I came here for the truth. I won't be leaving until I get it." She played her ace. "Where's your good-luck piece, Claude? Or haven't you missed your gold horseshoe?"

Claude frowned. "Gold horseshoe? I gave up on charms the day Breeze crippled me."

Breeze.

Leigh had almost forgotten the irony of Claude's riding a Fly Like the Wind colt the day of the accident. She hadn't been in Saratoga when it happened. But she'd seen footage. Had heard a dozen accounts.

The mean-spirited colt had been giving Claude a hard time from the moment he'd touched boot toe to stirrup. And late in the race, when Claude had used his crop on Breeze, the colt had gone berserk and slammed into a competitor. Both jockeys had been thrown, but Claude had been the one caught under flying hooves that severed his spinal cord.

She made some quick calculations, and suddenly everything fell into place.

"My God, Breeze had to have been a Wind Tunnel colt. That's it, isn't it?" She could read the truth in the face that looked older than it should have. He took a quick suck from the bottle as she continued. "And somehow you found out. You were trying to make Mama pay, to make us lose the farm. Only it was Jimmy who paid . . . with his life."

"Daddy isn't responsible for what happened," Desiree said from behind her.

Leigh whipped around to see her friend standing in the doorway dressed in jeans and Western boots and a fancy Windbreaker. She didn't look ready to race except for the twin braids of her flyaway blond hair that were tied together in back.

"Shouldn't you be at Keeneland?" Leigh asked.

"Car trouble." Desiree wore a worried expression. "I didn't get too far down the road when it plumb conked out. I came back here hopin' Daddy could drive me, but I see he's in no condition. Would you be a sugar and help me out, Leigh?"

Leigh could tell her friend was asking for more than that. For some kind of stay of execution for Claude. But she was *so close* to getting the truth out of the man. How could she stop now?

"Your daddy and I have been doing some serious talking."

"I know. I heard. Please, Leigh." Desiree's eyes pooled with tears. "I need to get to the track." She sighed. "And *I* can tell you everything you want to know."

"No, Desiree, don't!" Claude said anxiously.

"Daddy, don't worry. It's gonna be all right. You'll see. I'll make it all right." Desiree crossed the room to kiss her father on the cheek. Then she took the near-empty soda bottle from him. "Whyn't you go take a nap? Sleep'll make you feel better."

Claude began to cry silently. Tears rolled down his withered cheeks. "It's all over."

"I know, I know." She stooped in front of him and touched his cheek. "Please, Daddy, you worry me so when you drink. No more today, okay? For me?"

"I promise."

"And take that nap."

He didn't answer, merely stared after them as they walked out to Leigh's car. Desiree brushed tears from her eyes. A deep sadness filled Leigh. Her friend had been through so much lately. Now this—knowing her father had caused a man's death. How could Desiree think he wasn't responsible just because he'd probably acted under the influence of the alcohol?

They were on their way before Desiree began.

"Such a horrible thing, Daddy being stricken down in his prime, at the height of his career, to spend the rest of his days in that damn wheelchair. I tried to make it up to him. I moved back home. Took care of him. Rode my races for him. Turned down a chance to get married because of him. It wasn't enough. Nothing was enough to interest Daddy in building a new life. He kept growing more morose. When I finally caught him drinking himself into a stupor, he stopped trying to hide it from me."

"I'm so sorry."

Desiree kept going as though she hadn't been interrupted. "One night when he was falling-down drunk, Daddy told me about something he'd seen years before—Vanessa, Harley and Oakes switching studs. He'd been looking for Oakes and found him. What a surprise, huh? No one knew he'd seen, and he decided to keep it that way. He didn't approve of the deception, but Oakes was his best friend and Vanessa was one of the best owners to ride for."

Leigh could feel her friend's pain but could do nothing to assuage it. "I found out about the switch this morning. I was as shocked as you must have been."

And she'd been fooling herself when she'd considered protecting Mama. She'd told Doyle that her mother's crime hadn't hurt anyone. She hadn't counted on Claude. Not that riding a mean-spirited horse meant a jockey would get hurt any more than riding a good-natured one meant he wouldn't. It was the irony of the thing.

What would happen to him now? Leigh wondered. A man in his condition surely wouldn't last even a short stay in prison. "I wonder if Claude knew Breeze was Wind Tunnel's issue when he rode him."

"The thought never crossed his mind," Desiree said. "Not until I figured it out. That Wind Tunnel mean streak passed from sire to colt crippled Daddy!"

"If you believe that, why do you ride Typhoon? You must realize he's a product of the switch, too."

"But at least I know. I can choose to ride him or not. Daddy didn't have that choice."

Twisted logic, but Leigh could understand why Desiree was looking at the situation with her emotions. Her friend had devoted her whole life to complete her father's dream . . . just as she herself had.

The inadvertent comparison startled her.

"Claude sunk so low he figured getting revenge on Mama would make him feel better?" Leigh asked, gripping the steering wheel hard.

"What do you intend to do about it?"

"I don't have a choice, Desiree. I've got to tell the authorities everything."

"No! Please. I promise I'll fix things. The blackmail and threats will stop if you promise to help me cover up this whole mess."

"Are you crazy?" The words popped out of Leigh's mouth before she had time to think. That wasn't exactly the best approach with someone who was obviously emotionally overwrought. She glanced over at Desiree and was chilled by the jockey's expression.

"I was afraid you might say that," her friend whispered in a very unfriendly, steely voice.

Reaching into the pocket of her Windbreaker, Desiree pulled out a small but deadly looking gun.

Chapter Thirteen

"Hey, McCoy, good to see you back!" called Frank Harris, a rival handicapper from the *Lexington Dispatch*. "Where you been hiding yourself?"

"I've been around." Though he hadn't been in Keeneland's press room for days, not since the Blue Grass.

"Then I must've blinked."

With a chuckle, the man stopped at a desk equipped with a computer, FAX machine and telephone, and he placed a call.

Using binoculars to look through the plate-glass-windowed wall, Doyle saw the last of the horses that had been working out on the track heading for the tunnel on their way back to their barns. He'd barely gotten started, so the morning was a bust. When handicapping a race, he not only referred to past performances, but figured in his own observations about physical condition of a horse and, more important, response to the exercise rider during morning workouts. He kept his perceptions of daily sessions such as these in spiral notebooks.

But today, unable to concentrate, he'd done no more than doodle. He scowled at his rendition of a race-horse that looked more like a jackass and wondered if it could be considered a Freudian slip. Whatever.... He'd never make a living as an equine artist.

Workouts were finished, and early arriving fans were already claiming good seats for the afternoon's races. A little more than a week and Keeneland's spring meet would be over. And soon after, he knew many of those same fans would be crowding the grounds of Churchill Downs to watch the Run for the Roses—the Kentucky Derby.

That reminded him of Typhoon and High Flyer, both of whom had had serious workouts earlier, right after he'd first arrived at the track. Both colts were in top form, and he'd have a hell of a time choosing between them for the Derby...assuming nothing else went wrong.

And that reminded him of Leigh. He wondered what she was doing at this very moment. Was she playing amateur detective without him, and if so, would she think of him at all? He wasn't certain what a broken heart felt like—his relationship with Susan had deteriorated over a period of years, rather than in a single explosion—but he suspected this hollowness inside and the difficulty breathing were serious symptoms.

Frank got off the phone and sauntered over to where Doyle still sat facing the track. "How's it going?"

Looking down at his doodle, Doyle made a face. "I'm waiting to be inspired."

"The column could sure use it. Your predictions the past coupla days sucked big time," Frank said without malice.

His predictions *had* sucked. Other than playing the longshot Sugarman with Lamar, he hadn't called a single winner in days. "Can't win 'em all, I guess."

"Though the tribute to Jimmy hit home, huh? Maybe you oughta do more pieces like that—not that I hope we lose any more jockeys," Frank quickly added. "But you got the touch. You looked into the kid's soul. Too bad you couldn't do that with guys who are still around to appreciate it."

"Thanks, Frank."

As the other handicapper left the room, leaving Doyle alone, he had to admit his heart wasn't in what he was doing—except for the piece on Jimmy, of course.

Another thing to think about.

Reaching into the pocket of his sport jacket, he pulled out the photo he'd taken from his friend's album. Jimmy's joy at winning reached out to him. And to the other jockeys posing with him. They were sharing his first victory as if it were theirs, especially Claude, who had been Jimmy's ideal. The older jockey's silks were open and Doyle could see a gold chain dangling against his chest. Doyle would bet anything a magnifying glass would reveal a gold horseshoe charm at the end of that chain. All along, he'd had the evidence to link Claude to the good-luck piece.

Claude Walker. Doyle knew he had respected Jimmy, liked him even. So why hadn't he been at the hospital or at the wake? Because he was guilty? Or because he had evidence Keith was responsible?

Instinct told Doyle to keep looking, not to accept either explanation too easily, but the kind of thinking necessary to put the pieces together eluded him at present.

Because Leigh continued to haunt him.

Fool that he was, he'd never even told her he loved her.

DESIREE HAD FORCED Leigh to leave the car in a stand of trees on a side road behind Keeneland, and they were approaching the backside on foot. Leigh still had no idea what plan was fomenting in the jockey's mind, but of one thing she was certain. Unless she was able to get through to Desiree, each step brought her closer to the ultimate race, death to the loser. Talk about high stakes!

"You can stop now, Desiree," she said, eyeing the other woman, who walked a pace behind, right hand in her jacket pocket. "Jimmy's death was an accident. They'll only charge Claude with manslaughter, and considering the circumstances, he'll get off light. Maybe he can plead temporary insanity. He'd get help, and when he was better, he could start a new life."

Desiree laughed, and the sound sent a chill straight up Leigh's spine.

"Nothing can help Daddy. I know that now," the jockey said mournfully. "Still, I couldn't stand thinking about what happened to him and not acting. All I really wanted was to expose your mama and the men who helped her. To see justice done. But I didn't have proof. Daddy wouldn't stand by me. He was insanely loyal to people who were criminals. People responsible for ruining his life."

Leigh stumbled as, eyes wide, she turned to face Desiree. "You can't be saying what I think you are."

"Oh, I am, Leigh. I surely am. Daddy didn't blackmail your mama or drug your colt. *I* did."

Heart thundering, Leigh said, "But the horseshoe charm—"

"Daddy didn't wear it the day he rode Breeze. Maybe if he had, the accident would never have happened. I wore it for him. I rode all of my races for him."

"And you killed a man for him?" she choked out.

Desiree ignored the accusation. "When Vanessa ran out of money, I did things to the horses to make her know I was serious. I wanted her to mortgage the farm to the hilt. Just like happened to Daddy, I wanted her to lose everything."

"And me."

"You weren't ever part of the plan, Leigh. Honest. You should have promised to help me cover this up like I asked."

Desiree shoved Leigh to get her moving. Leigh stumbled forward half in a trance, not knowing if she could stand any more revelations for one day. Mama throwing away her ethics to keep someone else's dream alive. Doyle farther from her than ever. Desiree getting revenge for what happened to her daddy.

"If you didn't mean me any harm," she said, trying to concentrate on the road, "then why did you try to kill me in the pasture with Wind Tunnel? You didn't just knock me out—you dragged me into his path.''

''You were getting too close. I had to stop you. You had the note to Jimmy. Thane told me. I wanted it back and you shook up enough to make you stop.'' Desiree was talking as if she'd only tried to scare Leigh, rather than kill her. And she was talking faster, as if she were getting an adrenaline high from discussing her plans. ''I used the note to set up Oakes. I figured I could get them all at once with the drugging and the investigation that was sure to follow. Vanessa and Harley and Oakes.''

''And Jimmy?'' Leigh asked, mind whirling. ''What did he do?''

''I didn't count on Jimmy. He was my friend. I never meant for anything to happen to him, only for High Flyer to be disqualified if he won. Jimmy's death was a sad accident is all. I'll always blame myself for his death.''

Convinced that Desiree was sick, not evil, Leigh believed her. ''Then admit to it. You'll get help—''

''And I never would be allowed to ride again!'' Desiree shrieked. ''No state board would license me to get anywhere near a legitimate track.''

''There's lots of things you can do to work with horses.''

''No, this is better. Once I take care of you, I can stop, pretend none of this ever happened.''

Not wanting to specify Desiree's next victim, Leigh kept her words purposely vague. ''Too many people know too many things for you to get away with murder.''

"Murder? Who said anything about murder? You're about to meet with an unfortunate accident in your ex-husband's barn. If the authorities suspect anyone, it'll be him. That should make you happy."

At the moment, nothing was making her happy—except maybe if Doyle were to be spying on her as he had the day before.

Leigh recognized the irony of that wish. But it was the only way he'd know she was in trouble. He'd saved her twice, so why not a third time, when it really counted?

When did he listen to what she wanted him to do or not do, anyway?

If only she hadn't run out on Doyle earlier merely because he'd made her face some painful truths. Now she had more. Looking at Desiree, she could see what trying to live for someone else could do to a person. Twist them so that they couldn't tell right from wrong.

She'd been wrong to marry Keith to further her father's dream. Part of her had always known that.

As they got in sight of the Wingate Stud barn, she asked, "How do you expect to get away with this?"

"It's a perfect time, really. Workouts are over. Most everyone who can will be grabbing a quick lunch before the races start."

"Someone's bound to be around."

"Since Keith doesn't have any horses running today, there's probably no more than an assistant groom."

And Leigh had no doubts Desiree had already figured out how to get rid of *him*.

"Even if the shed row is deserted, someone nearby is bound to hear the gun."

Desiree merely laughed. The chilling sound sobered Leigh. Her lifelong friend really meant to kill her!

And if Desiree succeeded in her plan, so much was left hanging. If only she'd told Mama she understood and forgave her. If only she'd told Doyle she loved him. If only God would give her the opportunity to make amends with the people who meant the most to her.

If only she knew exactly what Desiree had in mind....

Too late to find out. They had arrived.

"Remember the gun and don't try to warn anyone. I'm certain you don't want someone else's death on your conscience."

But it didn't come to that. They circled the barn. Checked the office. Walked down the shed row. All stalls empty.

When they got to Typhoon's box, Desiree said, "In here."

Leigh stopped and stared at Desiree, at the madness in her eyes. And understood. Desiree wasn't worried about the gun making noise. She was going to let the tumultuous colt do her dirty work for her.

"Haven't we gone through this before?" she asked lightly as the jockey pulled aside the webbing across the opening. "All I got from Wind Tunnel was a couple of bruises."

"But this time I'm going to stick around to make sure Typhoon finishes the job." Desiree grabbed the bridle hanging outside the stall and shoved it at Leigh. "Put this on him."

"Why? Planning on riding him home?"

"I want it to look like you were the one tryin' to ride him when you had your unfortunate accident."

Clever. Nervously eyeing the high-strung colt, Leigh entered the stall. He immediately shied and faced the wall opposite.

Hoping to get Desiree off guard, Leigh said, "He knows you, not me. You'll have to do it."

"Not likely." The jockey pulled the gun from her pocket. "I can use an alternative plan, if necessary."

Leigh didn't need any more incentive. She spoke softly to the colt and ran her hand along his croup, then his back and finally his neck as she approached his head. When she was within reach, Typhoon whirled away, making her start over.

And Leigh saw her opportunity to stall—to look for an opening to get at Desiree's gun.

"So what did you do with the money you got from Mama?" she asked in a voice that would be pleasing to the colt.

"I haven't touched it. It's tainted. Made on a lie."

"I suppose you know why she did it."

"I don't care. All I need to know is what it did to Daddy."

Leigh realized there was no use in trying to convince her that Claude could have had the same tragic results from an accident on another horse. No jockey came away from the sport unscathed. Broken bones and concussions were practically as routine as the common cold.

Instead, she said, "You must really love him," and continued wooing Typhoon with gentle hands.

"Of course I do. Daddy was always everything to me, ever since Mama up and ran away on us when I was six. It near broke my heart when he recovered from the accident only to end up in that damn chair." Her eyes had lost that glint of madness; now they softened with collecting tears. "He was the best, you know. Better than Arcaro or Shoemaker. Cut down in his prime, and nothin' I could do."

"Just like my daddy," Leigh said, grabbing hold of Typhoon's halter. "Nothing I could do for him, either. But Mama tried to make him believe he had something to live for."

"He should have died," Desiree went on, and Leigh knew she was still talking about Claude. "I could give him everything but the one thing that was most important. I couldn't give him back his life at the track."

Leigh felt sorry for Desiree. How could desperation drive people to such lengths that they willingly became criminals? She wanted to reach out and take Desiree in her arms and tell her it would be all right. That everything would be fine. Just as Desiree had told Claude. But Leigh knew it would be a lie. The other woman had gone too far. Her mind had wandered too deep. And she was certain that Desiree could no longer distinguish right from wrong.

Leigh inserted a finger into Typhoon's mouth. His jaw popped open and she slid in the bit. The task went smoother than she ever would have guessed. Great. Now he was going to be cooperative so Desiree could murder her faster! Leigh had to keep the jockey talking and figure out a way to distract her long enough to get that gun away from her.

"You can't live someone's life for him, Desiree," Leigh said, not unaware that she was following in her own father's footsteps.

While fastening his halter, she surreptitiously pinched Typhoon and quickly backed away, so that when the irritated colt snorted and swung around, his head bobbed between them.

Desiree didn't seem to notice. "I don't know anything else."

"Maybe because you never thought you could have more." Leigh leaned against the colt, covertly elbowing him in the ribs until he shuffled his feet and nudged her in return. Wrong human! "You should have been a jockey for *yourself*, not for Claude."

As she should continue to work on the farm for herself. She loved being broodmare manager, she could never warm up to the business aspects of being farm manager as she could to helping deliver and care for a newborn foal.

"Daddy needs me," Desiree said defensively.

"Does he? Or is it you who needs him?"

"That's not true!"

Typhoon immediately picked up on Desiree's renewed agitation. He responded by throwing up his head and squealing, making Leigh realize she could use the jockey's anger to her advantage.

Necessity forced her to cruelty. "Maybe you don't want your daddy to have anyone else."

"You don't know what you're talking about," Desiree returned.

"Maybe you like him being in the wheelchair because then he has only you to depend on."

"I'm no monster!"

Typhoon quivered and his eyes rolled and Leigh slammed at Desiree's already fragile emotions. "You can't control which horses win, but you can control Claude, especially when he's hitting the bottle hard. Tell me, Desiree, are you getting the soda-pop moon for him?"

"How dare you!"

Desiree aimed the weapon at Leigh, and Typhoon went for her gun hand with lips peeled back.

"Hey!"

As his teeth sank into her arm, the jockey reacted automatically, lightly smacking the colt in the nose with her free hand...and giving Leigh her opening.

Before Desiree could recover from the distraction, Leigh lunged and caught the smaller woman in the breast with her shoulder, hands reaching for the gun.

"No-o-o!"

Blam!

Desiree's shout of fury followed by the gunshot incited the colt to terror. He screamed and reared, his hooves dangerously whispering along the length of Leigh's back as both women went over together onto the straw-laden floor. The shock of Leigh's weight landing on Desiree loosened the smaller woman's grip on the gun. Taking the advantage, Leigh bashed the weapon with a closed fist and sent it flying out of the stall and into the shed row.

They tussled in the straw, the colt dancing around them and protesting vocally. Desiree's clawed fingers came for her face. Leigh stopped her by grabbing the other woman's braids and twisting hard enough to tear out her hair.

"A-a-ah!" Desiree's hands ineffectually fought hers. "Let go!"

"Why?" Leigh's concentration was split between the two dangers—the snarling woman and the increasingly frenzied horse. "So you can kill me?"

Desiree turned feral, fighting Leigh with a strength achieved by a lifetime of athletic training. Leigh could barely keep hold of Desiree, and Typhoon didn't help when he clipped her in the hip hard enough to make her see stars—more bruises—and to let go.

Scrambling to her knees, Desiree made for the stall opening. And the gun. Equally desperate to keep her from the weapon, Leigh grabbed the jockey's foot and jerked as hard as she could. Desiree went down on her face, and Leigh scrambled over her body to block her escape.

The two women faced off, both panting, both sweating with the effort.

"Desiree, stop, please. Let me get you professional help."

"Too late to stop. I won't let them lock me up. I'd rather be dead."

Leigh wondered how much respite she had before Desiree would come for her again. As much as she hated firearms, perhaps *she* should go for the gun herself.

As if forgetting about Leigh, Desiree rose to her feet, softly clucking to the colt. "Typhoon, it's okay. It's me, baby. I won't let anyone hurt you," she crooned as she approached him.

Figuring the jockey was trying to make her let down her guard while preparing for a renewed assault, Leigh quickly calculated distance to the weapon. Typhoon danced, and Desiree followed his lead, magically calming him some. About to make her move for the gun, Leigh froze when, against all reason, Desiree grabbed both the leather reins and the colt's mane in her left hand and, in one tremendous vault, threw herself onto Typhoon's back.

"Desiree, what do you think you're doing?"

"What I do best!" Desiree yelled as the powerful colt surged forward.

Leaping out of the way lest she be trampled, Leigh thought fast. What to do? Desiree grabbed a whip from its peg on the wall and urged the colt to a trot. And Leigh knew she had to stop the jockey before she hurt the colt or some innocent bystander. Another horse— that's what she needed. Heading in the opposite direction, she flew out of the shed row and saw Micah leading a familiar bay toward the Wind Racer barn.

An unbelievable stroke of luck!

High Flyer was being brought in after training and cool down. Though his saddle had been removed, he still wore his bridle.

"Micah, wait!"

The wizened groom turned, his expression one of surprise. "Something wrong?"

She skidded to a stop at the colt's side. "Leg up."

"What?"

"Now." Leigh grabbed the reins from the groom's hands and lifted her left leg. Though she'd ridden bareback hundreds of times, she wasn't quite as athletic as the jockey.

"He's already been worked this morning," Micah protested, even as he caught her foot and gave her the boost she needed.

"I don't have a choice." She settled lightly on the colt's back and patted his neck reassuringly before turning him after Desiree and Typhoon. "Desiree drugged the colt!" she yelled back at Micah. "Call security!"

Leigh knew the chance she was taking. The colt's injuries were hardly healed. But when Desiree got Typhoon moving out, only one horse had a prayer of catching them. His mirror image. High Flyer.

Rounding the Wingate Stud barn, Leigh saw the other horse and rider. Desiree wasn't pushing Typhoon yet—she was keeping him at an easy trot, no doubt so she wouldn't unnecessarily arouse any suspicions. Then she glanced over her shoulder and spotted Leigh closing the gap on High Flyer. Even at a distance, Leigh could see the dementia overtake her friend again. Her face contorted, her body stiffened, and she screamed like a trapped animal.

In a last desperate flight for freedom, Desiree drove Typhoon straight for the racecourse itself.

Chapter Fourteen

Urging High Flyer into the paddock area, Leigh got help from an unexpected source. Doyle stepped out in front of Typhoon, spooking him from continuing straight for the tunnel leading to the track. The wild-eyed colt turned, and an equally frantic Desiree had to regroup.

"Desiree, stop a minute!" Doyle shouted as Leigh carefully guided High Flyer around arriving spectators and track workers who were stopping to gape at the unusual spectacle of two women riding bareback on thoroughbreds.

The jockey kept her mount moving in a tight circle until he'd danced a complete three-sixty, then aimed his nose at the tunnel again.

Doyle grabbed for the reins. "I have to talk to you about something important."

Desiree responded by screeching and cropping him away, then digging her heels into Typhoon's flanks, goosing him into the tunnel.

The short delay was all High Flyer needed to narrow the gap.

"Ash, what the hell's going on?" Doyle called as Leigh passed him.

She didn't stop, merely yelled, "Desiree isn't thinking straight," as she plunged High Flyer through the tunnel. "Get the outrider—and don't let her back through!"

The colt's hooves hitting the rubber brick created a muffled, spooky noise. When they broke daylight, Leigh spotted Desiree waving her crop to acknowledge the hundreds of early comers. Then she moved Typhoon down the track as if she were in a pre-race post parade. Leigh had no idea of what was going on in Desiree's mind, but certainly the jockey's perception had no resemblance to reality. She seemed to have forgotten she was being followed.

The realization that Desiree had really lost it chilled Leigh, and she collected High Flyer into an easy trot.

The jockey was an even greater danger than before, with her mount as her weapon. Typhoon was straining at the bit and sweating profusely. Not a good sign. He was picking up on bad vibes and he was a difficult ride at his best. Somehow, she had to talk Desiree off Typhoon before the disturbed woman had a chance to bring the horse to harm.

When Typhoon bucked and twisted, High Flyer threw up his head, snorting and prancing.

He was ready for a match race.

A thrill shot through Leigh. She'd taken High Flyer, as well as dozens of other colts and fillies, around the farm's practice track, but she'd never worked out on a real racetrack, and certainly not without a saddle. The element of risk would be high not only for her, but for the colt. Thinking it might be best to block the tunnel opening until reinforcements arrived so that Desiree would have no escape route—and surely the woman would tire of this game eventually—Leigh tried to turn High Flyer.

But the colt balked. He was determined to run. She tried again. He fought her, putting Leigh in a quandary. Using force wasn't the best idea, either.

"Desiree, wait for me."

The other woman glanced back. But before Leigh could catch up, the jockey dug in her heels and lay low over Typhoon's neck. He immediately shot forward, galloping like a bat out of hell.

"Desiree!" she yelled, but her old friend refused to acknowledge her.

Without warning, High Flyer broke fast, following in Typhoon's wake.

Now Leigh had no choice but to let him run. Maybe they could catch Desiree before reaching the tunnel. Maybe Leigh could stop her. She took the first turn with her heart in her throat and her knees clamped tight against the colt's barrel. She prayed to keep her seat. Somehow she managed it, finding renewed balance along the stretch.

Ahead, Typhoon had a lead of at least a dozen lengths. Beneath her, High Flyer ate the track easily. Leaning farther into his neck, she gently squeezed her legs and he picked up tempo.

The dozen lengths shortened to ten. Seven. Five.

In the distance behind them, she heard a shout and another set of hooves. The outrider! Help at last!

Ahead, Desiree glanced at them by looking back under her arm as jockeys did during a race. In response to the closing gap, she used the crop on Typhoon, who immediately gathered muscle and powered forward.

And Leigh knew this was it. This race was for real. Nothing else would satisfy Desiree.

Approaching the second turn, she said, "C'mon, Bad Boy, let's catch your cousin," and urged him with her legs.

High Flyer fired, and miraculously Leigh clung to him without lying flat against his neck as she was tempted to do. They were on the stretch. A half-dozen lengths became three. Then two. Once more Desiree glanced under her arm. Once more, she touched the crop to Typhoon's hindquarters. Her colt responded valiantly.

Hands gripping the reins on either side of High Flyer's neck, Leigh used a scrubbing motion to urge him faster.

Though she heard the hoofbeats pounding close behind her, she couldn't chance looking back to check on the outrider's position. She brought High Flyer around Typhoon on the outside so Desiree couldn't veer off and take the tunnel.

The next thing she knew, they were neck and neck, dueling for the finish line in a dead heat.

"Desiree, stop, please!" Leigh shouted, daring to take her eyes off the track for a few seconds. "Give up before it's too late!"

Face contorted in fury, Desiree yelled, "Never!"

In a desperate attempt to stop the jockey before she ran Typhoon into the ground, Leigh reached out for his reins and was rewarded with the crop slashing at her arm over and over. A panicked Typhoon shrilled and jerked away from the violence. And as that extra set of hooves thundered up behind them, Desiree lost her seat.

Typhoon dodged toward the rail, leaving Desiree suspended in midair between horses for a second, before she plunged to the track with a high-pitched, haunting howl.

A sickening lurch told Leigh that High Flyer hadn't been able to avoid trampling the downed jockey. Another set of hooves behind finished the job. And now ahead, Typhoon was running wilder and faster with no guidance or weight on his back. Suddenly another thoroughbred shot past her, and the uniformed outrider reached for the riderless colt, easily securing the reins as he was often forced to do in actual competitions.

The race to the death over, High Flyer slowed on his own. By the time Leigh was able to get him in hand and trot him back around in a half circle, a dozen people scattered over the field. They converged on Desiree's still form, which lay on the track like a broken doll. Doyle was among them. A couple of track employees on ponies dismounted. One rushed to look for vital signs. People swarmed around Leigh, asking her questions. Unable to understand what they wanted of her, she stared blankly through them.

Then she sought out Desiree—a pitiful, twisted sight not unlike Jimmy had been—and was thankful when ranks closed around her friend so she wouldn't be compelled to continue looking.

Suddenly, she was aware of hands dragging at her waist. Doyle. He was helping her dismount, setting her on her feet, circling her with his arms.

Micah came puffing up. "I'll take the Bad Boy here and cool him down."

Leigh nodded. Her throat was too full for her to speak. Her legs shook, and she knew that without Doyle's support, she would surely collapse. She licked her lips, tried to form the question, but the words wouldn't come.

He shook his head.

He didn't have to say it. She knew.

Another jockey dead . . . and this time she was responsible.

"YOU'RE NOT RESPONSIBLE," Doyle told Leigh for maybe the tenth time.

Not having left her side all afternoon, he'd heard her story over and over—she'd told it to track security, to Win Kenney, to the local authorities and, most recently and devastatingly, to Claude Walker. Back at Wind Racer at last, ensconced in the living room, sipping at a brandy, she'd shared the horrible news with her mother.

"Doyle's right, Ashleigh, darlin'," Vanessa said, sitting next to her daughter and patting Leigh's knee. "Desiree was a fine jockey and a fine young woman, but somewhere along the way, her mind tumbled over an invisible edge. Perhaps dealing with Claude was too much of a burden for her to cope with."

Color was flooding back into Leigh's cheeks from the brandy, but she held on to the glass with such force that her knuckles whitened. "She said she never accepted what happened to him."

"He never let her," Doyle insisted. "He didn't have to give up on life because he was confined to a chair.

All that talent and knowledge of horses wasted. So many people in the industry admired and respected him, he could have started a new career, maybe as a trainer. But he chose to feel sorry for himself, and in the end, his refusal to accept his loss and rebuild destroyed them both."

Leigh seemed to take heart from his words, yet she still protested. "But if I hadn't chased her...trapped her...Desiree might be alive. We could have gotten her help."

"And she might have hurt or even killed someone else—Typhoon included," Vanessa said. "Life is full of 'what ifs.' If I hadn't switched stallions, Claude might not be in a wheelchair."

"You can't know that."

"Any more than you know Desiree could have been saved." Vanessa rose. "You're a very brave young woman, Ashleigh, and I'm proud to have you as my daughter."

Leigh set down the remainder of her drink and stood. "And I'm proud to have you as my mother."

They threw their arms around each other, and for a moment, Doyle thought they would both start weeping. But then Vanessa pulled away with a sniff and stroked Leigh's cheek.

"I think I shall find Harley and Thane and bring them up-to-date. We have some serious decisions to make about the future."

As did he, Doyle realized.

"What decisions, Mama?"

"About how to handle revealing our guilt in switching the studs, among other things."

"You're willing to do that?" Doyle's respect for Vanessa grew.

"I must. I cannot put my daughter in the position of feeling like she has betrayed me."

"How did you know?" Leigh's question was guarded. "I had had thoughts of keeping silent."

"But you wouldn't have. I know you, my love. It's time I was as brave as my own daughter."

Vanessa left quietly, leaving Leigh staring after her.

"Are you all right?" Doyle asked. "Can I get you anything? A doctor?" He'd suggested her being checked over before, but stubborn as she was, Leigh wouldn't hear of shirking her responsibility in clarifying Desiree's death to those most concerned.

"A shower and a good sleep will do wonders," she said. "Though I'm not certain the second is possible."

"I can stay and tell you a boring bedtime story that will put you to sleep."

She almost smiled. "I'll be fine. Don't you have a column to write?"

He nodded. A column about Desiree. Frank Harris's suggestion he do more columns like the one on Jimmy stayed with him. Although he hadn't been overly fond of Desiree Walker himself, he had understood her.

"That can wait," he said, "if you need me."

"I do need you, Doyle McCoy," she said somewhat shyly. "To love me like I do you."

"Hey, I'm crazy about you." He loosely circled her with his arms. The light in her eyes touched him deep inside. "But two people need more than love for a relationship to work, Ash."

The light flickered and dimmed. "They need to be from the same side of the racetrack?"

"Among other things."

They certainly had differences to work out. Or he did, mostly, Doyle thought. "We need to take a break from each other."

"A break." She pushed at his chest until he let go of her. "Right," she said sarcastically. "We've been getting along far too well, so a break would be best."

He could see she didn't think that at all. He was tempted to relent, to tell her everything would work out. A lie. Until he figured out how they could be happy together, not just with each other but with the outside forces that affected a relationship, he didn't see any point in them torturing themselves by pretending.

"We've had a common goal," he said. "A purpose that brought us close, made us work together. Without that..."

"...there's nothing," she finished for him. "Of course. You go on now. I'm tired."

And forlorn-looking. So sad she looked about to sink into the floor. Doyle weakened. "Oh, Ash, I wish you could understand."

"Please!" She held out her hands as though they could protect her from more hurtful words. "The sooner we go on with our own lives, the better."

Right. The better for both of them. But the decision didn't satisfy him on any level. On the way back to the car, Doyle cursed himself.

For crushing Leigh's hopes.

For doing nothing to mend his own heart.

DERBY DAY. Nothing like it. After a week of nonstop activities that kept Louisville and Lexington and all the farms in between jumping—parades and steamboat races, public concerts for the masses and private parties for the rich and famous—the first Saturday in May had arrived.

"Are you sure you don't want to join Vanessa and your friends?" Harley asked.

Watching Micah giving High Flyer a little last-minute spit and polish from the shed row, Leigh said, "I'm not taking my eyes off this Bad Boy here until he's on his way through the tunnel."

"Suit yourself," he said without animosity.

She and the trainer had silently declared a truce. Cleared of the drugging charges, Harley Barnett was back on the job. At least temporarily. Another investigation was under way concerning the improprieties of switching studs. Since the racing commission had never dealt with a situation of this magnitude before, no one could guess the outcome. As far as criminal charges were concerned, the statute of limitations had run out.

That did not mean there would be no consequences to the business or to the individuals involved. The truth was out. Public. Some people understood. Others didn't. The future of Wind Racer Farm was murky.

And the problem sat heavily on Leigh's shoulders. While still majority owner, Mama had abdicated her role as head of the business. Now Leigh was doomed to become farm manager when Thane retired in the fall. The responsibility pressed down on her. But what choice did she have?

She still wanted what was best for the farm, if not in the same narrow-focused way as before. Zeroing in on a dream to the exclusion of human feeling was all wrong. Look how many people had been disappointed or destroyed by her father's and Claude's dreams already.

"Heard a rumor this morning about McCoy." Leaning on the stall wall next to her, Harley interrupted her thoughts.

Prepared for a nasty diatribe, Leigh clenched her jaw and remained silent.

"I was talking to Rey Boudreaux, giving him last-minute tips on how to handle High Flyer if he gets caught in traffic. One thing led to another.... The next thing I knew we were talking about the 'unpleasantness.'"

Normally a euphemism for the Civil War. God knew she felt as if she'd been through a war, starting with the Blue Grass disaster. And the skirmishes hadn't yet ended.

Harley went on. "Well, seems McCoy made a big donation to the Disabled Jockeys Fund in Jimmy's name."

"How big?"

"Thirty-thousand-dollars big."

"Thirty..."

The winnings from the long shot. Doyle hadn't continued betting as she'd feared. He'd given the money away, and in Jimmy's name! The knowledge lightened Leigh's sadness a bit. Something good had come from all the bad.

"What made you think I'd be interested?"

Harley snorted. "It's written all over you, missy."

In the past week and a half, she'd spent a lot of time thinking about Doyle's decision to leave her. A break, he'd called it. If only that were true. If only she could figure out a way to lure him back to her, to make him believe that she at least saw them as equals and that was all that need concern him. She suspected he had more pride than that.

Then again, his giving the money away proved that he could change....

Doyle McCoy was pushed out of her mind by the reality at hand. It was nearly post time for the most prestigious race in the country. She accompanied Harley and Micah and High Flyer to the paddock area. Churchill Downs was one of the oldest racetracks in the country. There were newer. More polished. But nothing set her heart aflutter like the twin spires that were recognized the world over in the thoroughbred racing industry.

The Kentucky Derby was a media event. Scores of people had camped outside the grounds all night. By eight that morning, when the gates opened, the numbers had swelled. Nearly one hundred and fifty thousand people from across the country were already partying inside, mostly packed in the infield. As was traditional, many wore creative—if sometimes startlingly bad—hats and held Derby souvenir glasses filled with mint juleps.

A few thousand crowded the paddock area, as well. Fans who didn't have seats and would watch the race as they had all the others that day—on the screen above the paddock stalls.

Just outside the paddock area, the horse identifier checked the tattoo on the inside upper lip of each thoroughbred. Once passed, the colts were saddled, then the colors and markings also checked by the identifier. Finally, the animals were led into the walking ring, and the jockeys entered.

Snugged to the closest rail, people who had been waiting in place for hours to see these equine heroes oohed and aahed. In the center of the ring, owners, friends and celebrity fans gathered not only to see their prize horses, but to be interviewed by the press and to be oohed and aahed over by the crowd, as well.

Leigh told herself that she was not disappointed she couldn't find Doyle among the press. So why did she keep looking for those rugged features and that dark chestnut hair? What would that do but hurt?

"Riders up!" announced the paddock judge.

The simple words shot a thrill through Leigh. This was it. The once-in-a-lifetime chance that only twenty of all three-year-old thoroughbreds per year experienced.

Harley gave Rey Boudreaux a leg up on High Flyer.

Keith did the same for Victor Medina on Typhoon.

The two favorites, both with new jockeys, both having raced their hearts out barely two weeks before. Normally horses of this caliber were raced no more frequently than every three or four weeks. Some Derby contenders did not go on to the Preakness, because the second leg of the Triple Crown didn't give them enough time to rest.

Leigh prayed she'd made the right decision for High Flyer. Harley said he was sound. She had to learn to trust Harley sometime.

The jockeys urged their mounts to the tunnel, fans calling out to both horses and riders. Strains of "My Old Kentucky Home" filled the racecourse and everyone stood in tribute. Harley followed Leigh to the clubhouse and the Wind Racer box where Jennifer, Harmony and Nolan were keeping Vanessa company.

And where another familiar profile startled her.

As if he sensed her presence, Doyle found her in the crowd, an enigmatic grin slanting his lips. He was dressed in a beige suit and a purple shirt that almost matched the color of her dress. His tie was a yellow and purple silk not unlike the band decorating her broad-brimmed hat.

If this was some kind of ploy...if he thought he could worm his way back into her life without groveling a little...he had another think coming.

"Doyle McCoy, isn't it a little hot for snakes to be crawlin' out from under their rocks?"

"Ashleigh!" came her mother's shocked response.

But Doyle grinned. "Why, Ash—open hostility? I do believe you've missed me."

She'd sooner walk over a field of horse pats barefoot than admit it. "Why aren't you in the press box?" she asked instead, inwardly demanding her respiratory and circulatory systems to return to normal.

"Change of venue" was all he said.

She stared at him blankly, not understanding, as Harley pushed her into the box and to the empty seat next to Doyle. Glancing at Mama, she suspected she'd been set up. Even her friends smirked at her as if they knew something she didn't.

The last strains of "My Old Kentucky Home" died down and everyone sat. On the field, the jockeys cantered their mounts in tandem with the ponies whose riders had decorated their manes and tails with flowers and ribbons.

"Why so fancy?" she asked of his unusual outfit.

"I thought it would be appropriate."

"How so?"

"I made Vanessa an offer to buy half of her share of Wind Racer. Pending the bank's approval for a loan . . . and your agreement, of course."

Leigh blinked at him stupidly, then looked down to the track where horses were being loaded into the chutes of the starting gate. One balked—Typhoon, of course—and had to be pushed in by two assistant starters.

"You want to buy into the farm?" She forced the question through stiff lips; jumping to assumptions was merely asking for more hurt. "Why?"

"I quit my job as a handicapper. And while I've talked my editor into giving me a try writing profiles on people in the racing industry, I need some kind of backup in case it doesn't work out."

His sensitive piece on Desiree had surpassed the tribute to Jimmy. He'd revealed her anguish and her guilt, her outrage and her mistaken quest for justice. Reading it had made Leigh cry.

"You quit your job?" she echoed as the starting bell clanged.

Over the loudspeaker, the announcer called, *"And they're off for the Kentucky Derby!"*

"I faced facts," Doyle said, leaning close so only she could hear. "Someone with a gambling problem shouldn't be playing with the odds for a living."

A burst of happiness flooded her and she met his eyes. "Oh, Doyle!"

He firmly turned her head back to the racetrack. "Watch, or you'll never forgive me when you miss your colt win."

The horses were approaching the first turn, and as Leigh might have expected, both High Flyer and Typhoon were solidly in the middle of the field.

"Dangerous shows early speed," called the announcer. *"Good Vibrations tucked in at the rail and coming up fast...."*

"I don't understand," Leigh said, leaning toward Doyle while watching the race through binoculars. She had to know his motivations. "Why would you *really* want to buy into Wind Racer?"

"I forgot the pleasure of working with horses until we teamed up." He teased her ear with his warm breath and a promise. "If we were partners, in fact, we'd both be part of the same side of the racetrack."

Leigh grinned and her heart soared. He was trying to work things out. He really did love her!

"It's Good Vibrations... Dangerous falling back... Still Waters in third place and gaining...."

The crowd rose as one, and Leigh set down the binoculars. Mama stood in front of her. She placed a hand on the older woman's shoulder and received an encouraging pat. Whatever the outcome of the Derby, Leigh knew she would remember this day forever.

She slipped her free hand in Doyle's and squeezed. "Welcome, partner," she whispered.

"They're tightly packed as they move to the top of the stretch. High Flyer is closing stoutly in the middle of the racetrack... Typhoon is right there with him...."

Doyle threw his arm around her waist and pulled her close as the field made the second turn.

"And down the stretch they come!" yelled the announcer. *"Good Vibrations in the lead, Still Waters a*

*close second.... High Flyer begins to roll on the out-
side... Typhoon finding his way to the rail.*"

"He's gaining," Nolan said.

And the normally decorous Harmony yelled her encouragement. "High Flyer—do it!"

"Here goes," Leigh said, her chest so tight she
couldn't draw a deep breath.

"*Typhoon is passing Still Waters on one side...High
Flyer on the other.*"

"Yes!" Jennifer squealed from behind her.

"C'mon, Rey!" Harley shouted. "Give that colt a
goose like I told you!"

"*Good Vibrations is dropping back.... It's Typhoon by a head, High Flyer second...*"

Typhoon's head hung low as usual, and as High
Flyer inched forward, Typhoon seemed about to go for
him.

Leigh held her breath.

"*They're neck and neck.... It's Typhoon and High
Flyer with Good Vibrations a clear third.*"

Somehow, without using his crop, Rey Boudreaux
got High Flyer to focus forward.

"Go, Bad Boy, go!" Leigh's scream was echoed by
voices around her, most appreciatively Doyle's. "*Typhoon and High Flyer... Typhoon and High Flyer...
and they're under the wire together!*"

The crowd roared as the look-alike colts crossed the
finish line in tandem.

Mama was screaming and hanging on to Harley.

"*A photo finish! Hold on to your tickets while the
judges make a determination.*"

"Omigod, I can't stand it!" Harmony complained.

"How about you?" Doyle asked Leigh.

"I can stand anything if I don't have to do it alone."

"I'm glad you approve of my offer to Vanessa."

"I was hoping there'd be one to me, too."

"I'm not an expert on working directly with thoroughbreds like you are, but I work hard and learn fast," Doyle said. "And Vanessa tells me you hate dealing with uncreative things like books and inventory. As you know, I'm a whiz with figures."

Though she felt the burden that had been pressing her already lifting off her shoulders, Leigh demanded, "A more personal offer!" because she wanted it all. Someone with whom she could build a whole life, not just a business.

"Fair enough," Doyle agreed. "I want us to start over, without prejudices. A clean slate."

"What are the odds on our making it together?" Leigh asked.

"I don't do that anymore," he reminded her.

"I'm not asking for a professional opinion. I want a personal one."

"Working together will give us a chance to really know one another. We may have some things to work out, but I've never met a couple who didn't. I think we can lick anything together. So what do you say?"

"*Ladies and gentlemen,*" the announcer interrupted, "*it's a good thing Churchill Downs keeps a second gold cup in its vaults. For the first time in the history of the Kentucky Derby, we have a dead heat!*"

"We won!" Vanessa cried.

"We really did." Leigh laughed through her tears as she became the center of a group hug.

No matter that her colt hadn't beat Keith's. She hoped the results of the race would go a long way toward making people forgive the switch of stallions, for while High Flyer was descended from Fly Like the Wind, Typhoon came from a Wind Tunnel mare, proving that there were no absolutes when it came to breeding.

And that went for people as well as for horses.

Leigh threw her arms around Doyle's neck. "I'm ready for whatever life you have to offer. But then, I've always known we belonged together, ever since I was thirteen."

"Stop gloating and let's go get your prize."

But as Leigh headed the small parade to the winner's circle, she knew Doyle had already given it to her.

HARLEQUIN®
INTRIGUE®

HARLEQUIN INTRIGUE INVITES YOU TO

A HALLOWEEN QUARTET

Celebrate All Hallows' Eve with four couples who battle things
that go bump in the night—and emotions that have a life of
their own. Ghastly ghouls and midnight trysts abound in these
four Halloween romances from your favorite Intrigue authors.

In November, look for them . . . for the scare—and the love—of
a lifetime.

HALL-W

1993 Keepsake

CHRISTMAS

Stories

Capture the spirit and romance of Christmas with KEEPSAKE CHRISTMAS STORIES, a collection of three stories by favorite historical authors. The perfect Christmas gift!

Don't miss these heartwarming stories, available in November wherever Harlequin books are sold:

ONCE UPON A CHRISTMAS by Curtiss Ann Matlock
A FAIRYTALE SEASON by Marianne Willman
TIDINGS OF JOY by Victoria Pade

ADD A TOUCH OF ROMANCE TO YOUR HOLIDAY SEASON WITH KEEPSAKE CHRISTMAS STORIES!

HX93

HARLEQUIN®
INTRIGUE®

"I AM BETRAYED"

In the still of the night, those were the words spoken to Emma Devlin by her husband, Frank... from beyond the grave. She'd given him no cause to doubt her devotion, yet he haunted her waking hours and disturbed her dreams.

Harlequin Intrigue brings you a chilling tale of love and disloyalty...

#241 FLESH AND BLOOD
by Caroline Burnes
September 1993

In an antebellum mansion, Emma finds help from the oddest of sources: in the aura of a benevolent ghost—and in the arms of a gallant Confederate colonel.

For a spine-tingling story about a love that transcends time, don't miss #241 FLESH AND BLOOD, available now from Harlequin Intrigue.

Relive the romance...
Harlequin® is proud to bring you

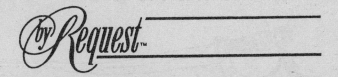

A new collection of three complete novels every month. By the most requested authors, featuring the most requested themes.

Available in October:

DREAMSCAPE

They're falling under a spell!
But is it love—or magic?

Three complete novels in one special collection:

GHOST OF A CHANCE by Jayne Ann Krentz
BEWITCHING HOUR by Anne Stuart
REMEMBER ME by Bobby Hutchinson

Available wherever Harlequin books are sold.

Calloway Corners

In September, Harlequin is proud to bring readers four involving, romantic stories about the Calloway sisters, set in Calloway Corners, Louisiana. Written by four of Harlequin's most popular and award-winning authors, you'll be enchanted by these sisters and the men they love!

MARIAH by Sandra Canfield
JO by Tracy Hughes
TESS by Katherine Burton
EDEN by Penny Richards

As an added bonus, you can enter a sweepstakes contest to win a trip to Calloway Corners, and meet all four authors. Watch for details in all Calloway Corners books in September.